A VILLAGE MURDER

by

Carola S. Goodman

To My World – Docta Jory, Gabriella C., Marissa R., and B.Jory

Copyright © 2010 by Carola Goodman
Los Angeles, California 90036
All rights reserved
Printed in the United States of America

Chapter 1

"I'd like some nice hot scones, some of that delicious chocolate cake, a couple of Napoleons, oh, and please don't forget the creamed horns," said Susana to the ship's server. "It's so nice being on a ship that has such a talented chef. Isn't it?"

"Yes, madam!" replied the server with an amused expression.

Susana Leslie sat in an overstuffed armchair looking expectantly at the entrance of the tea lounge. She sat wondering if this was her seventh, or was it her eighth crossing on the luxury cruise line. It was always a surprise to her that the ship's staff knew her by name. She would have been amazed to know the extent they went to assure that her trips were pleasurable.

When the waiter arrived at her table carrying a three-tiered tea, she expectantly asked him if he had seen her sister, Cornelia.

"I distinctly remember her telling me to meet her here for tea. I know it's somewhat early for tea - it's only three o'clock. Isn't it? Oh dear, I know Cornelia was emphatic about that time. Wasn't she?" The waiter smiled and pretended to dust invisible crumbs from the table. He was quite used to Susana's caprice of ending sentences with a question.

Susana forgot her anxiety when she saw the appetizing pastries set in front of her. She really should watch her weight but a few pastries couldn't hurt, she told herself. After all, she had been taking exercise by walking twice around the deck every day since the ship sailed out of New York. And now it was only a couple of days before they reached Southampton.

She continued her conversation with herself, "Really, why Cornelia should be so fussy about having tea at this hour and then not bother to show up is beyond me, isn't it?"

Just as she was soothing her nerves with a nice plump, creamy eclair she heard the unmistakable footsteps of her older sister. It had always seemed to Susana that while Cornelia was the elder by only sixteen months there was an ocean of difference in their maturity. While Susana played house and dressed her dolls, Cornelia preferred to run about outdoors until dinner time.

Before Cornelia spotted their table Susana took the last Napoleon and daintily managed to stuff the entire pastry in her mouth. Food - especially French pastries – had always been her downfall. And by the look on Cornelia's face, she would need this extra nourishment.

"That dope of a brother of ours just sent me this email!" Cornelia pronounced handing Susana her cell phone. "It was my understanding that we were going to meet at Blandings to discuss the donation of land," she continued.

"Oh Cornelia, do sit down, everyone is staring at us, aren't they?" replied Susana. The dot of whipped cream on the end of her nose gave credence to her plea. Susana continued, "Yes, I believe we are scheduled to meet with the vicar and the town selectmen regarding their little dilemma of not having enough land for those on their way up – or is it down?"

"Well our brother has decided that as he puts it, 'we'll kill two birds with one stone' by having a gourmet feast prepared by the 'Premier Chefs of London'!" replied Cornelia, her face having gone a bright puce.

"Why what a charming, not to mention, delicious way to entertain all our friends!" exclaimed Susana casting a forlorn look at the mini chocolate cakes. If she took one, Cornelia might think she wasn't paying attention and then go on her usual rant of 'too many sweets blah, blah,blah'. She might even call the server to clear the table! No, no she must keep a concentrated, interested expression. In this capacity she furrowed her eyebrows and pouted her mouth in a hopeful imitation of concentrated thought telling herself that she really was thinking – just not about her brother's email. Instead she was concentrating on the menu for the gourmet feast.

"Susana!" hissed Cornelia. "If you insist on not wearing your glasses then please get contacts. That myopic stare is going to drive me crazy! Really, what can that fool of a brother of ours be thinking?"

"Oh but Cornelia, a nice, gourmet dinner prepared by classically trained chefs would be lovely don't you think? I mean Martha is very nice and her chocolate chip cookies *are* delicious - at least when she gets the recipe right, but I really don't think we can compare her cooking with that of the 'Premier Chefs of London', can we?"

Cornelia muttered something under her breath. Then, in a controlled voice said, "Susana, food is not the issue here. And it's not going to be just a nice, cozy family affair. Jack's invited the vicar and Julia along with the entire board of selectmen!"

Susana had lost interest. She was lost in thought about her favorite pastime. "I always think a family dinner with a nice rib roast with mashed potatoes and sauteed spinach or a big bowl of soup served with garlic bread is *so* comforting. Of course a really delicious dessert can transform any tasteless dinner, don't you agree? Although Martha never seems to..."

"Haven't you been listening? Will you please stop talking about food for one second and think what this will do to our donation!" pleaded Cornelia. "You know how villagers love to gossip! Everyone will know that we intend to donate some of our land to the town for use as a cemetery. And believe me, not everyone will be pleased."

Epping was a small town located in the county of West Sussex in the south of England. The Leslie family home known as Blandings was situated in the older and historic center of Epping known to the locals as 'the village'.

"Oh I'm not so sure. It really was such a good idea of Julia's. She really is very clever - although one would never think it to look at her. Life is full of funny little oddities isn't it?" Susana sat back with a puzzled expression on her face.

Cornelia was not listening. She had her eyes fixed along the horizon thinking about the meddlesome politicos who ran Epping. No doubt they would all want a voice as to how to use the land. The sisters and their younger brother held British and American passports. Their English mother had met her American husband during the war. The three

7

Leslie children were born in the States but had spent the majority of their childhood at 'Blandings' their mother's ancestral home overlooking the village of Epping. The summer vacations were spent with their American relatives. The Leslie children had inherited an equal share in the family estate. Having married Americans Cornelia and Susana lived mainly in the United States and after many decades of marriage had been widowed within a year of each other. Early on it had been decided that Jack should live at Blandings full time and oversee the management of the manor and extensive grounds.

It had been the custom in the month of June for Cornelia and Susana along with their husbands to sail from New York to Southampton for the summer. This particular crossing was unique in that it was the first made as widows.

A large wave hitting the starboard side jolted the sisters out of their separate reveries. There were small cries of surprise by some of their fellow passengers who rose from their seats and attempted to head for the exit as the ship rocked. Susana and Cornelia, being seasoned sailors, waived off the offer of assistance by the ship's staff and remained leisurely composed in their seats.

"It looks like we're finally going to have exciting weather!" exclaimed Susana. "I do hope the passengers won't be too sick, don't you?" Then almost in the same breath she continued, "Dinner is still hours away, shall we order more tea?"

Chapter 2

The following day was the last day of the crossing and Cornelia was already at breakfast when Susana came in to join her.

"Wasn't it lovely last night?" asked Susana breathlessly even before sitting down, "There's really nothing like a good storm out at sea to help one sleep. Don't you think so, Cornelia?" She sat down and assumed an expression of sophisticated detachment that lasted thirty seconds before she jumped out of her chair and practically ran to the gargantuan breakfast buffet. She returned to the table delicately carrying two plates.

"Since today is the last breakfast aboard ship I thought I might as well enjoy these delicious eggs and sauce Bearnaise. I love how they put asparagus in the sauce - do you think I over did it?"

"Not at all," chuckled a resigned Cornelia.
A server quickly appeared at Susana's side nervously looking at her balancing act. "Don't trouble yourself, Hans. I've had plenty of practice. The smoked salmon looks devine – please don't let those scrumptious brioches at the buffet disappear will you?" She looked at Cornelia who sat with only a cup of coffee in hand.

Knowing what her sister was thinking, Susana

said, "I'm starting my tomato diet tomorrow so I'm trying to fortify myself now - isn't it all so yummy?" A tiny bit of sauce Bearnaise quivered on her chin.

Cornelia looked on with amused tolerance while her sister enjoyed her food because she appreciated the fact that Susana was a world-class chef in her own right. It was not unusual for her to host dinner parties for twelve guests with five courses that she had personally prepared. Her reputation as a gourmet chef was well known.

"I'm glad you had a good night's sleep, Susana, but while you were dreaming I was racking my little grey cells trying to think of a way to downplay our donation to the village. I keep thinking of the harassing questions we're going to get from those nosey, interfering, no-gooders. If only Jack hadn't blabbed about the donation before we arrived and then arranged a dinner as a 'formal announcement'," she sighed in frustration.

"Cornelia, you worry too much. Everyone will know about the donation eventually - oops, why is it that when food falls from my fork it always misses the napkin?" replied Susana dunking her napkin in water and rubbing her white slacks. Getting back on topic she continued, "Jack meant no harm, he just loves people and parties. Besides, we're giving a charitable donation and surely that can't make anyone angry. Oh, by the way, I've also been racking my brains – about the dinner - I've decided that the menu should be extra special don't you?"

Cornelia sat back silently wondering if Susana had it right. After all, it was common knowledge that the *'village telegraph'* aka *gossiping locals*, made it nearly impossible to keep anything secret in Epping.

That afternoon they arrived in Southampton

and from there they boarded a train for the next leg of their journey. As so often happened, once they left the city and entered the countryside, the landscape brought back memories of happy times spent in this part of the world.

Cornelia looked out on the English meadows and felt a rush of pleasure. They had arrived in time to see the English Autumn with all its bounties. Gold and scarlet sailed past their windows. This was a busy time for farmers when they spent a large part of their time in their tractors harvesting produce and gathering hay before the onset of winter. The train passed by fields bordered with hedgerows with contentedly grazing cows. Cornelia thought of the countless little creatures that made these hedgerows their homes. The trees in the autumnal sun glowed with glorious ruby, scarlet and orange colors some of them massive and hundreds of years old. Every once in a while a church tower was seen. All these were familiar and comforting sights for the two sisters.

"It's close on to four o'clock Cornelia," said Susana anxiously, "Do you think they'll wait tea for us?"

"We're only about a thirty minute drive from the manor. I don't think we'll miss tea completely and if we do, we'll just ask Martha to make up a new batch. Besides, Jack knows we're arriving this afternoon so he's probably told Martha to have everything ready and waiting."

"Oh," Susana chattered excitedly, "I do hope so, you know how much I dislike doing without my tea. And after all, we are in England and tea does taste so much better here don't you think so Cornelia?"

At last they arrived at stately Blandings. Once

inside the gates a path bordered by plane trees lead up to the stone nineteenth century manor. As the car swung in front of the house Jack emerged from inside. He gave his sisters a warm, brotherly welcome and with arms through those of his sisters, he guided them to the front door. Before they entered, a young woman stepped out and smiled brilliantly at them. The sisters stared at the woman and then simultaneously looked at their brother.

"Perfect timing ladies, tea awaits us in the library. Susana, I had Martha order those 'Maids of Honor' from the Tarts and Buns especially for you. The roses had a fantastic run this summer, Cornelia. In fact you won't believe the show of late blooming roses!"

"I'm eager to see them," replied Cornelia. Then turning to politely smile at the young woman said, "Jack, you're forgetting to introduce us to your guest."

"I'm so sorry," Jack rushed up to the young woman and holding her by the arm brought her to his sisters,

"With all the excitement of seeing you I quite forgot about introductions! Cornelia, Susana, allow me to introduce Betty Smith." Bestowing a lovelorn look at Betty, he continued, "Betty's become a very important person in my life."

At that precise moment, as if on cue from the gods, a huge clap of thunder made an announcement of its own kind. It wasn't clear which decree caused the embarrassing silence that ensued. Susana was the first to react. She approached Betty and hugging the young woman gushed, "But this is so thrilling! We're going to absolutely love having you in the family! Do you like to cook?

Unused to Susana's facility of introducing various unrelated topics in one thought Betty managed a shy smile in reply.

Cornelia had more difficulty swallowing this latest news and even more difficulty trying to smile. She loved her brother and there was nothing in the world that the she wanted more than to have him happily married - happily married to someone whom they all knew. Still too shocked to ad lib, she took her cue from Susana and gave Betty a quick hug while looking at her sister and saying, "Susana I think you're jumping to conclusions," and then with less frostiness than she felt continued, "Betty you must tell us all about yourself as soon as we have a moment." Then turning to Susana and giving her a meaningful look she said, "We've had a long day of traveling and I really think we need to freshen up. When we come down we can show Jack what we brought him from New York. Are you coming, Susana?"

"We brought him something?" asked Susana looking puzzled.

"We'll be right down Jack." Cornelia continued hurriedly, "Shall we meet in the library for tea in a few minutes?" Reaching the front staircase, the sisters went up in dignified silence. The rigidness of Cornelia's back and the lack of chatter from Susana were sure signs that an ill wind blew at Blandings.

When they reached the second floor landing Susana grabbed Cornelia's arm and with a look of hurtful resentment asked her if she had known of Jack's engagement. "Is that why you gave me those looks down there Cornelia?" she asked, "I always thought Jack would marry someone close to the family and well..." Susana wavered, "Betty is very pretty and she does seem to have a charming personality but..."

Cornelia interrupted her, "No one has said anything about an engagement, Susana. But if they did, don't you think I'd have told you?" she hissed trying to keep her voice down as they made their way down the long corridor to their rooms. "Jack seems to be doing everything in his power to annoy us and he's doing a first rate job of it." Entering her old room she continued, "We have five minutes to figure out what we're going to do when we go back downstairs. We can't confront Jack about the dinner party with a stranger present."

"Oh isn't it lovely being back here," asked Susana as she looked around Cornelia's room decorated in soft yellow tones. Before Cornelia could bark at her, Susana rambled on, "Maybe we can talk to Jack when Betty leaves...Ohhh....", she suddenly clasped her hands to her chest and stared at Cornelia.

Knowing her sister's penchant for the dramatic Cornelia replied with admirable resignation, "What in the world is wrong now?"

"It just occurred to me that maybe Betty is staying here. Do you think?" queried Susana. Her anxious expression faded to a kindly smile as she continued, "Of course that could be very pleasant. We'd be able to really get to know her. Right?"

"Finding out if she's a permanent fixture here won't be a problem," responded Cornelia with determination.

"Exactly. Well, we can't let Martha's efforts go to waste - can we?" Susana headed for the door and tea.

"Didn't you want to find out whether Betty is

staying here?" whispered her sister.

Susana turned and in a soothing voice as if speaking to a not very bright chimpanzee said, "Well of course! We'll nonchalantly ask her when we see her downstairs. Good idea?"

"Much easier to just find the room!" answered a frustrated Cornelia already heading out the door. "We have less than two minutes to find it so come on!"

With a sigh and a tortured expression Susana followed Cornelia back towards the guest bedrooms in search of Betty's room. Confident that everyone was downstairs, Cornelia entered the first two rooms without knocking. They found Betty's bedroom on the third try.

"Well now, she's very neat and tidy - don't you think we should go?" asked Susana anxiously looking at the door afraid that Betty might open it at any moment.

Cornelia was barely audible as she rummaged through the walk-in closet, "We have to look in the closet and her bureau to see how much clothing she's brought so we know how long she plans to stay!"

"I really don't think this is very nice of us, after all, Betty is..." Susana's voice trailed off as she heard the bedroom door open and in walked Martha holding a comforter.

"Susana, come here and look at this!" bellowed Cornelia. "She has enough clothes here to last her 'til...oh my gosh...look at all the shoes! I don't think I've ever seen this many shoes in one place!"

A forced high-pitched laugh emerged from Susana's throat and in a theatrically loud voice asked, "Cornelia, did you find your missing golf shoes? I'm sure Martha here could help us look for them.

Couldn't you Martha?"

"I guess so," mumbled Martha staring wide-eyed at the closet. Cornelia, with casual aplomb sauntered from the closet. "Martha..." she began, "...so nice to see you. I can't for the life of me find my golf shoes have you seen them?"

With a suspicious look, Martha answered, "'Course I 'ave - they're in your closet. Same as always."

"Oh...those are my old ones - hurt my feet. And besides, I've brought new ones." Cornelia noticed with dismay that Martha, who was normally slow on the uptake had a quizzical look on her face. Martha Jenkins had been born and bred in the village of Epping and knew everyone and everything about everyone. It was common knowledge among the villagers that she was a believer in the occult and maintained that she had 'second sight'. She had started out as a kitchen maid for the Leslie family but with the economic downturn she had been retained as housekeeper/cook.

The sisters left Betty's room under Martha's watchful stare. "What rotten luck. I thought that loony Martha was preparing tea in the kitchen." whispered Cornelia, "Now she'll be spreading stories around the village that we rummage through other people's closets."

Susana looked confused, "I believe we *were* rummaging through someone else's closet. Weren't we?"

"Oh let's go downstairs," answered an exasperated Cornelia. "It's enough that we're going to have to deal with Martha's idiotic 'clairvoyance' and those crazy eyes boring into us."

When they approached the library they heard

laughter coming from inside. They entered and saw a roaring fire in the fireplace and Jack sitting on the arm of a sofa with his head leaning towards Betty.

"What took you two?" he asked as he escorted both to a sofa in front of the fireplace, "If you're worried about missing your tea, don't be. As usual, Martha can't keep to a schedule so you haven't missed anything."

With a worried expression Susana replied, "Maybe she needs some help in the kitchen?" Turning a nervous look at Betty she continued, She isn't terribly organized you know. Shall I go see if I can help?"

"Susana, do sit down. I'm sure Betty won't mind going into the kitchen to assist Martha," suggested Cornelia with a smile that would put the Cheshire cat to shame.

Jack nervously looked at Betty who remained comfortably rooted in her chair. Then springing up from the arm of the chair he hastily replied, "I know how to handle Martha. Be back in a jiffy."

"No Jack, I'm sure Betty is more than capable in the kitchen," his sister insisted, "Betty please go and see if Martha needs assistance."

"Anything to please," retorted Betty as she slowly uncrossed her legs. With an equally forced smile at Cornelia she rose and exited the room.

"Did you have to be so nasty," asked Jack once Betty had gone. "You've just arrived and already you're starting in on her."

Susana chimed in, "You were just a teensy weensy bit bossy. Weren't you?"

Cornelia's steady voice remained calm. "In case you've forgotten, tomorrow evening we have an assembly of people when we make the formal presentation to the village. Don't you realize that we need to prepare for the questions that will surely be asked?"

"And what does that have to do with Betty?" asked Jack.

His sister raised her hands and let them fall into her lap in an expression of frustration. "Jack, none of us know a thing about Betty. This is the first time Susana and I have met her. We can't possibly have a family discussion with someone about whom we know nothing."

"Cornelia's right, Jack. Does she like staying here?" asked Susana in her muddled way.

Jack looked at his sisters and asked, "How do you know she's staying here?"

"Well all the clothes in the bureau and closet, oh and the shoes, weren't there a lot of shoes Cornelia?" volunteered Susana.

"What? I can't believe you two not only entered Betty's room without asking but then proceeded to go through her things!" said Jack in amazement.

Her brother's look of disbelief had the effect of making Susana stammer and sputter. "We were only checking that she was being made comfortable, isn't that right Cornelia?"

Cornelia had the dignity to blush as she looked down at her folded hands.

Any further discussion was interrupted as Betty entered the library followed by Martha pushing a tea trolley loaded with an assortment of sandwiches, small iced cakes, bread, butter, and the specially ordered 'Maids of Honor' pastries. Susana immediately sat upright and motioned to Martha that she would pour the tea. Martha sniffed and pushed the trolley next to Susana while Betty slid cozily alongside Jack.

"Now tell us all about yourself Betty. This really is a surprise that Jack played on us you know. Have you known each other long?" Susana smiled warmly as she passed Betty a cup. "This is such a wonderful place for romance. I remember when Jack was a teenager and we'd come out for the summer, he'd have..."

Before she could continue Jack hastily broke in saying, "Betty is here as a substitute teacher at the elementary school. I met her when she took her class for a hike along the footpath on the north side of the estate. Remember that old oak tree we used to climb at the edge of the path? Well, I was trying to help old Spooner with the pruning of a precariously overhanging branch when along came Betty with her charges. It was love at first sight," then quickly added, "At least for me."

The awkwardness was broken by a shrill scream. Jack was the first to run out into the hall with the women close on his heels. The screaming had stopped but the sisters and Betty all huddled behind Jack.

"Oh my, gosh, who's making that racket?" asked a frightened Susana.

"Take a wild guess. It has to be Martha of course. She's the only other person here," replied Cornelia with admirable resignation.

With Jack in the lead, they quickly made their way to the kitchen.

Chapter 3

When they pushed open the kitchen door, they found Martha holding on to the back of a chair and staring at the wall in front of her. "Martha! What is it?" shouted the sisters in unison.

Jack walked up to Martha and prying her hands off the back of the chair turned her around and sat her down.

Martha continued to stare in front of her. Cornelia and Susana looked on in alarm while Betty had an expression of abject terror.

"I think we need to call Dr. Goodman. Don't you?" asked Susana. Jack bent down in front of Martha and with his hands firmly on her shoulders asked, "Martha, what's happened? Has something frightened you?"

"I know where it's 'idden," said Martha in a faraway voice while not looking at Jack..

Susana let out a tiny scream and her sister gaped at Martha. They could not see Betty who was standing behind them, her hands clasped tightly in an effort to keep them from shaking.

Then all at once, Martha jumped out of the chair and with a suspicious look at everyone headed for the sink and began to wash dishes with furious determination. The siblings stared at each other with questioning expressions until Jack blurted out, "Martha, can you tell us what's hidden and where?"

"Know? 'idden? I don't know what yur talkin' about," declared Martha.

"But Martha, you said all those funny things just now! Don't you remember?" blinked Susana.

"I told you I don't know what you're talkin' about! I'm washin' dishes ain't I? Can't I git on with my work without you all crowdin' my kitchen?" grumbled Martha attacking the dishes and splashing soapy water all over herself, the counters and the floor.

Perceiving that they were not going to get an explanation, Jack signaled the others to leave. As they filed back into the library, Susana said, "Oh dear, she's really not feeling well. Don't you think we should call Dr. Goodman to check on her?"

Without waiting for an answer she sat down and loaded her plate with pastries. "Ooooh, it's all I can do to finish my tea but I really think I have to keep up my stamina. She's so nutty isn't she?"

"Of course! She's wackier than a loon – always has been. That scene in the kitchen was the latest manifestation of her 'second sight'," replied Cornelia.

Betty spoke for the first time, "What do you mean by 'second sight'? You don't really mean she has ESP?" she asked with a forced attempt at laughter.

"Oh we don't think she's got ESP, no, no, nothing like that," smiled Susana daintily biting into a cream puff. "But she has been right on the mark about a few things in the past. Hasn't she?"

Cornelia snorted, "I can't remember her having a catatonic episode before. At least I never witnessed one. Her M.O. is usually a prediction of something dire given to us just as we're seated for dinner. She loves an audience."

Betty laughed nervously and said, "These country bumpkins are so quaint with their old lores and beliefs. There's really no absolute scientific proof that people can predict or see the past or future."

That evening, dinner at the Leslie household was late owing to Martha's barely remembering to put the roast in the oven twenty minutes before the customary dinner hour.

Throughout dinner Susana maintained a constant nervous chatter in an attempt to keep the flow of conversation going unaided by the others who were too distracted pondering the events of the day.

Early the following morning, Cornelia came down the front staircase headed for the kitchen to make the morning coffee. As she came to the last step, she was relieved to hear Susana humming in the kitchen, a welcome sign that the coffee that morning would be palatable. The household had learned early on that Martha could not be relied upon for kitchen duty, or for that matter, any duty until ten o'clock in the morning.

"Good morning, you're up unusually early," Cornelia greeted an apron clad Susana as she reached for the coffee pot. "What's in the oven? It smells heavenly."

Susana, who had been icing cinnamon rolls fresh from the oven looked up and said, "Since this is our first morning here I thought I'd make us all a nice breakfast. Yes?"

"Cinnamon rolls! Ooh, they look yummy!" replied Cornelia leaning towards the rolls and inhaling the delicious aroma appreciatively.

"There's farina on the table if you'd like that to start. Oh, and I made a pancetta and potato fritatta and I found some nice sausages in the fridge that grilled up beautifully," said Susana excitedly as she whirled around the kitchen moving from stove to ovens making Cornelia's head spin.

Cornelia helped herself to farina and sat down at the kitchen table, "I didn't sleep a wink last night thinking about tonight," she said as she poured heavy cream over the farina.

As if on cue Jack entered the kitchen in his robe expressing his joy that Susana was taking charge of breakfast.

"Mmm, a real breakfast! Martha's coffee is like drinking freshly made sludge. The last time I tried to make myself some food she grabbed her broom, which incidentally I think she uses for transportation, and followed me around until I couldn't stand it any longer and left her to it."

"When Betty comes down we can all sit down and eat. Alright?" suggested Susana, carrying heaping platters to the table.

"We can sit down to breakfast right now. Betty won't be down until lunch time." replied Jack hungrily eyeing the sausages and fritatta.

"But didn't you say that Betty taught school?" asked Susana, "Isn't there school today?"

Jack was quick to reply, "I said she was a substitute teacher. The regular teacher was out with a sprained ankle but she's back now."

"Sounds to me like Betty enjoys her creature comforts. But in this instance I consider it lucky because we can now comfortably discuss tonight's schedule. What time are we to expect the onslaught?" asked Cornelia.

"Susana, there's no one that makes frittatas like yours. They're better than at Rome's Hotel Hastler!" said Jack avoiding Cornelia's stare.

"Don't change the topic, Jack. Please answer my question," insisted an irritated Cornelia while admitting to herself that he was right about Susana's cooking.

"Hmm, let me think," replied Jack aware that he was in dangerous waters and stalling for time.

"I know that the chef from the Culinary Foundation will be here at four o'clock with his crew. I'm so excited! You don't mind if I wear my apron over my evening dress do you?" Seeing the impatient look on her sister's face, Susana quickly added, "After all it is quite one of my fancy aprons. Isn't it?"

"And what time are the guests due to arrive and how many are there?" Cornelia once again asked her brother.

"Really, darling you always look stunning and you have a wonderful sense of style all your own but don't you think the apron thing is a bit much?" asked Jack hoping to forestall Cornelia.

"J-A-C-K!" growled his older sister.

"Alright, you don't have to shout at me. I was about to answer you," he replied with an innocently. Fighting for time, he wiped his mouth with precise movements and then with the flair of a matador placed the napkin on the table. "Let's see now, I believe everyone's arriving at the usual time – cocktails at eight and dinner at half past. Happy now Cornelia?"

"Oh dear," sighed Susana looking down at the second roll on her plate.

"What's the 'oh dear' for?" asked her brother calmly, "We always eat at eight thirty."

"It's not that, Jack – I was just thinking about the time Julia got up on the table to demonstrate her flamenco skills. Do you remember how she almost broke her neck?"

"Of course I remember. No one who was at that party will ever forget her dancing," laughed Jack.

Cornelia had to wipe the tears from her face as they recalled the disastrous events at a party given in honor of the library's bicentennial and the inebriation of the vicar's sister, Julia.

"I don't think she'll ever live that one down!" Cornelia managed to say between gulps of air.

Jack responded, "It's common knowledge that Julia's now a complete teetotaler and lectures to one and all at every opportunity. She's the kiss of death to any party so her poor brother's hardly ever invited anywhere."

"Isn't that too dreadful?" gasped Susana.

"Thank you for getting us back on track," replied Cornelia sarcastically. Then with a withering look at Jack asked, "For the hundredth time, who exactly will be coming tonight?"

"I must say that I have to agree with Susana. The situation is definitely dreadful. In fact it's *distressingly* appalling," announced their brother as he endeavored without success to hide a crooked smile, "At the top of the guest list are the Reverend Peters and his ogre…I mean his sister, Julia. I've been wracking my brains trying to come up with a plan to keep her away.

Bestowing an adoring look at her brother, Susana replied, "Don't worry, Jack, I can manage Julia. Can't I?"

It was Jack's turn to look amused and he continued, "To round out the guest list, or should I say casting call..." and he proceeded to list the invitees.

Chapter 4

Although the family would have preferred to have cocktails served on the terrace overlooking the gardens, the fickle English weather did not cooperate. By late afternoon it had turned windy with ominous dark clouds covering the sky. Cocktails would have to be served in the solarium where one could still look out onto the gardens while enjoying the benefits of central heating.

With the arrival of the chef from the prestigious Culinary Foundation, Susana disappeared to the kitchen and was not seen again until after the arrival of the first guests.

At a little before eight o'clock in the evening, Cornelia entered the solarium to find Jack already with a drink in his hand. Betty had had to go to town directly after lunch and it was Cornelia's firm hope that she would not return. "Is Betty back?" she delicately asked Jack who had gone to mix his sister a cocktail.

"Not yet – probably lost track of time shopping," answered her brother trying his best to sound casual.

Dressed in flowing chiffon inadequately covered by a wispy apron Susana fluttered around the army of cooks, looking over shoulders, effusive with admiration and approval. Succumbing to her gushing praise, the chef had conferred upon her the title of 'honorary sous chef' for the evening, a title which she used to her advantage taking endless samples at every cooking station.

Martha had been relegated to her own station with her favorite task – peeling potatoes. Susana kindly made it a point to praise Martha's speed and agility with the paring knife.

"T'ain't nothin', I can peel ten 'taters in under two minutes!" responded Martha with pride. Sadly, this was not news to the family as Martha's roasted potatoes had a striking resemblance to '*Tatertots*'.

The Reverend Thomas Peters and his sister Julia were the first guests to arrive and were grudgingly conducted to the solarium by a sulking Martha who had been hastily handed a clean apron and prodded to the front door to await the arrival of the guests. The vicar, who had been established in the parish of St. Mary's since time immemorial, was greeted warmly.

"It is entirely our pleasure to come to your lovely home and to thank you in person for the very charitable gift that you're making to the village and town," stated the vicar in his soft, tremulous voice. "There's no way to get around the fact that as mortals we must have a final resting place. I know it will be most gratefully received."

"Nonsense, we haven't any use for that section of land, might as well donate it to a worthy cause," replied Jack as he took the vicar by the arm and guided him to an armchair. "Now what can I get you to drink?"

"Oh, whatever you're having will suit me fine," responded the vicar a little self-consciously.

Jumping in front of Jack, her lips spread into a thin line in a caricature of a smile, the vicar's sister, Julia said, "Jack, you know I don't permit Thomas to drink alcoholic beverages at home."

"Yes Julia we all know that but since you're not at home..." Jack's attempted reply was interrupted by Susana, who, sensing that her brother was ready to do battle on behalf of the vicar, picked up a pitcher of lemonade and said, "Julia dear, you must taste this lemonade. The lemons in the greenhouse are gigantic and so sweet and juicy. Have a glass?"

What sounded like someone hiccuping followed by laughter could be heard coming from outside. The party in the solarium turned expectantly to look as two women walked in from the terrace.

Phyllis Stavis was a dark, hearty, big boned woman who had a reputation for being jocular and intelligent. She held the position of superintendent of schools for the village of Epping and also held the title of chairwoman of the 'Friends of the Library', the commission which controlled the funds for the library. Her partner, Debra O'Neil was a demure, plump blonde and an accomplished author of children's books. Her shy demeanor expressed itself by hiccups whenever she was nervous. The women were fond of entertaining and hosted monthly bridge parties in a charming cottage on a side street off the village common.

"Sorry we came in through the terrace – no answer at your front door," laughed Phyllis.

"That's odd, I stationed Martha at the front door. I wonder what she's up to. That woman can't follow a single instruction," replied Cornelia shaking her head.

"Not to worry, I'll go find her. Julia, want to

come with?" Susana practically pulled Julia out of her chair.

"That looney is probably sloshed in the broom closet. I don't know how you put up with that nitwit," replied Julia sententiously as Susana propelled her towards the front hall. The doorbell rang just as they got there.

On opening the door, Susana became even more distracted than usual and began to nervously pat her hair. "So nice to see you, Sam! Did you happen to run into Martha?" she asked the distinguished looking man smiling down at her.

Sam Taylor was a prominent and successful local farmer whose status as a bachelor weighed prominently in the minds of several females who considered him the 'best catch around.' His strong good looks, mild temperament and simple demeanor were the cause of many a female heart flutter.

Sam replied, "Thank you, Susana, very nice to have you and Cornelia back in the village. I hope you had a pleasant voyage." Looking around he continued, "So Martha's disappeared aye? I came up the road from east of the village and I didn't run into her but she could have cut across through Hunter's Bosk. Seeing the distress on Susana's face he continued, "Don't worry. She'll turn up. Martha's lived here all her life and knows this country better than most." He said this with a charming smile. Looking out into the distance his expression changed, "I thought he was away," he added to no one in particular.

Susana followed Sam's gaze and saw a nondescript fellow wearing wrinkled khaki pants and a corduroy jacket walking up the gravel drive.

"Oh how silly of me, that was one of your

jokes - wasn't it?" She waived to Moe Stone who, like Sam, was a member of the Epping board of selectmen the body that governed the town.

Julia, never one to stand in the background, hurried to meet Moe and said, "So glad you considered it your duty to join us. I know everyone will be interested to hear about how we intend to use the land." Then with a venomous look at Susana, stated, "That is if they stop pouring alcohol down everyone's throat!"

It was well known in the village that Sam Taylor had strong views on land use often opposing a majority of town officials whom he considered officious land grabbing charlatans. Sam was aware of Moe Stone's tendency to vote in concert with Julia's wishes. He had been born and raised on his farm and had strong feelings that not only his property but the entire village should be protected against outside developers. There had been many village meetings where Sam was outspoken about the actions of certain people who had purposely bought property only to turn around and sell it to outside contractors and developers. Sam had gained popularity amongst the residents when, as a newly elected selectman, he had exposed the misrepresented and fraudulent sale of a swamp to the village for the purpose of building a secondary school. From that point on it had been merely a matter of time before he became chairman of the board of selectmen.

In the solarium, Jack leaned against a potted palm with one eye on the door expectantly waiting for Betty to arrive.

"How many of these have you had?" asked Cornelia noticing his bloodshot eyes and pointing to his glass.

"I'm not keeping track but thank heavens for these plants, they're coming in handy - and don't think they're holding me up. I'm using them as shelter from that gargoyle." replied Jack casting a baleful glance at Julia. Cornelia rolled her eyes upward and turned to speak to Sam who had suddenly appeared at her elbow.

"Thanks for the invitation, Cornelia, I hear we're going to have a gourmet feast. Makes me feel like part of the in-crowd," he joked smiling with his eyes.

"Actually this was Jack's idea," replied Cornelia. In reply to Sam's raised eyebrows she quickly added, "But of course Susana and I joined in the planning."

"Word has it that you'll be donating some of your land to the town. That's mighty generous of you but I hope you've thought it through," he winked at her and walked over in the direction of the vicar.

Julia, seeing that Sam was heading towards her brother, made a beeline from her position of attack at the drinks table and overtook his approach. With a sweeping glare at those in the solarium, she remarked caustically, "I've been keeping my eye on all of the drinking that's going on here. It's absolutely disgusting how some people with positions of influence imbibe the devil's punch."

"Do you have firsthand knowledge of that?" asked Sam trying to keep a straight face.

"Are you blind? Can't you see how the alcohol is pouring from those bottles?" replied Julia completely immune from the barb. "If they weren't going to be giving that piece of land to us, that is the town, I'm sure I wouldn't have accepted their invitation to this drunken orgy," she continued gaining speed. "Look at how they've used this so called meeting to force my brother into debauchery!"

Sam, with visions of the vicar and his fellow guests in a pornographic x-rated film was unable to keep down a chortle of laughter. "I hardly think the vicar is at risk of compromising his orders," his voice quavered in an effort to hold back laughter.

A loud gong was heard at half past eight. A few seconds later the doors of the solarium opened and a somewhat disheveled Susana burst into the room to announce that dinner was served and to superfluously ask if everyone had heard the dinner gong. She had taken off her apron but was still in possession of a large wooden spoon.

Aware of the astonished looks on the faces of her guests, Susana managed to explain in a mildly shrill voice, "I was in the midst of folding egg whites into warm chocolate when I realized that it was eight thirty and that the dinner gong had not been rung. Looking around the room she said, "I wonder where Martha is? It's a good thing I still had this wooden spoon because the mallet for the gong is missing - anyone seen it?"

Cornelia, taking control of the situation asked Jack to take the guests into the dining room.

By this time, Jack had come to the conclusion that Betty had skipped and was not coming back. He alternated between accusing his goofball sisters of intimidating Betty, and thereby causing her escape, and relief at not having to be continually on stage in her presence. Just as he was pulling a chair out for Julia, he noticed out of the corner of his eye a white floating cloud swish into the chair next to his. He looked over just as Betty's exotic perfume enveloped his nostrils.

Jack immediately felt both disappointment and relief while Cornelia sent daggers in Betty's direction. Planting a kiss on Betty's cheek, he said, "You look smashing! Did you buy that in London?"

"Um...yes, do you like it? The traffic was terrible. I hope I haven't caused anyone to worry," she replied as she lifted her glass of wine with shaking hands.

Susana approached Cornelia and whispered in her ear. "What do you think we should do about Jim?"

Jim McCarthy was the editor of the *'Town Crier'*, Epping's only newspaper. He also worked overtime as the paper's investigative reporter and photographer.

Cornelia looked over at the vacant chair between Susana and Phyllis. "Isn't he here yet?" she asked, "What with trying to keep everyone from strangling Julia during cocktails I completely forgot he was invited. He's probably detained with some news copy. I think we should leave his place setting just in case he shows up," she continued eager to get on with the evening's agenda.

Julia, seated between Debra and Jack, clicked her tongue as a server began to pour wine. "Why bother with food, they might just as well give everyone a bottle and a straw," she quipped maliciously, "How in heavens a proper announcement will be made is beyond me when the entire group minus one is in an alcoholic stupor." Moe, catching wind of where this was going, immediately put his hand over his wine glass in a signal to the server that he was abstaining.

Chapter 5

As the evening progressed, Julia's disapproval continued although her appetite suffered no ill effects. Casting a malevolent look at Betty she said, "Really Jack, you should watch over young Betty, she's almost under the table with drink."

Betty, who had worn a wary expression the entire evening, looked up but before she could speak Julia continued mendaciously, "Betty dear, you're not at all looking well. Is your complexion usually that blotchy?"

"My dear!" voiced the vicar, too shocked to say anything else.

"Julia, it's about time that someone..." started Jack.

"Please, please!" interrupted Susana, "We are all here as friends and neighbors. I won't have anyone spoil this evening! Now, please, I implore you to not act like spoiled children. Will you?"

All but one had the grace to look embarrassed in response to Susana's admonishments.

Julia looked at her hostess and with an amused chuckle said, "Dear Susana, always so innocuous! Sometimes I wonder if anyone can really be that vapid."

Despite Julia's efforts the dinner was a great success with the guests enjoying each other's company not to mention the epicurean delights. Susana was in her element, explaining the nuances of each dish as the guests listened and ate with expressions of pleasure. Before long, the dishes had been cleared and everyone eagerly awaited dessert. Susana's penchant for sweets carried into her culinary talent. The chef had given her the honor of preparing the evening's dessert. With each course, he had come out to explain the dish prior to its being served. He now appeared and asked Susana to stand as her dessert was placed on the sideboard to the "oohs" and "aahs" from the guests. With the chef's assistance, Susana began to serve the creme caramel when there was a loud noise out in the hall followed by sounds of bumps and thumps along the walls. The sounds came nearer and nearer until the dining room door opened with a crash. Martha stood leaning against the door while holding on to the doorknob for support. As she slowly peeled herself away from the door, a red gooey streak trickled down one side of her face and a large bump could be seen slowly but colorfully forming on her forehead.

As if on stage Martha hobbled her way to the center of the room amidst squeals, murmurs and a couple of exclamations of horror. Her audience remained frozen in their seats while Susana, paralyzed with shock and dread, remained glued where she stood while shakily holding a dessert dish which was slowly oozing its contents onto the rug.

Martha, eyes boring into her audience and arms twisting her apron into knots asked, "Which one of you pushed me? I know it was one of you! 'Oo pushed me down the cellar stairs?"

"Try to sit down, Martha, you've blood all over your face," said Jack taking her arm and gently guiding her to a chair.

"Is that what's dripping all over our lovely Persian rug?" asked Susana in stunned shock.

"Don't you touch me! I know it was one of you!" flashed Martha, as she continued to stare at the stunned faces in the room.

"Goodness Martha! We must get a doctor to examine your head!" pleaded the vicar, barely dodging a fall as he hastened to come to her aid. Then, realizing that what he said might be misconstrued, he hastily added, "You must have hit your head when you fell and we should check that you don't have a concussion." Still holding his napkin he helped her into the chair. Dipping a corner of the napkin into a glass of water he proceeded to wipe her face.

"It's not right, pushin' nice people down cellar stairs. I coulda' been killed!" continued Martha as the vicar's shaky hands managed to get more water on the tablecloth than on her face. "Hey! Watch what yur doin'! I don't mind your tremblin' paws on me but I'm gonna have a dickens of a time gettin' the water marks off this 'ere table if you don't stop makin' this mess!"

The guests stared in fascination as Martha jumped from her chair, grabbed napkins off laps and began an industrious cleaning of the table.

Julia bent her head towards Moe who had suddenly appeared next to her and with a stage whisper said, "She's mad and I'm sure she reeks of alcohol!"

Wondering what it would take to permanently clobber Martha, Cornelia approached her and taking hold of her arm, gently but firmly escorted her out of the room.

As the door closed behind them, the guests, in an attempt to establish normalcy, but making a bad job of it, all spoke at the same time.

"I didn't know we were going to have entertainment with dinner!" laughed Phyllis somewhat unkindly in her booming voice. "Martha's such a scream!"

"She's a character alright, but that lump looked like it hurt. She might need a doctor," volunteered Sam.

"Martha's very highly strung," added Susana gravely. "I really hope no one pushed her into the cellar – it's a little scary down there isn't it?"

"I'd like to know what she was doing in that part of the house. Wasn't she supposed to be by the front door?" asked Julia.

"Maybe someone...hiccup...in the kitchen asked her...hiccup...to get something," hiccuped Debra.

"The fall must have affected her mind," began the vicar shaking his head sadly. Then thinking it over continued, "I mean she must have lost her footing and fallen down the stairs. I can't believe that anyone would harm the poor woman."

"Well from the beating she gave the table, it doesn't look like she's any worse for wear," quipped Phyllis, "Let's finish off this excellent Cabernet and drink to Martha's good health!" she gave a jolly laugh as she handed the bottle to Julia.

Forcing a tight lipped smile which had the appearance of a grimace and through clenched teeth Julia replied, "Thank you, Phyllis, I'll take your offer in terms of a social grace but I refuse to imbibe as I believe the purpose of this evening was to discuss an important event for the village," she continued sententiously, "I guess I'm the only one here who cares a twit about the village. If I had known that most of the evening's activities would be centered around a bottle I would not have bothered to come."

"Oh come now Julia," blinked her brother, "You know all of us here care deeply about the village. It's not a sin to enjoy good food and the company of others."

"Your brother's right, you know," replied Sam, "All of us are here with one purpose in mind. Of course the excellent meal provided by our hosts is an added pleasure. There'll be plenty of time to discuss serious business later."

With a spiteful look aimed in Sam's direction, Julia replied, "Now I would have thought that you, Sam, would be the first to want to get down to business. Doesn't the land being proposed for donation abut your farmland?"

Aware of a sudden silence in the room she continued, "And come to think of it, you've always been so adamant about keeping land out of the hands of developers. It seems to me that you've not been very forthright."

"Why does that sanctimonious old cow always have to put a damper on things?" remarked Phyllis to her end of the table. "The poor vicar can't go anywhere without her trailing behind him."

"I feel sorry for him," whispered Debra, "It can't be any fun always having her around." Then turning to see that Julia was looking at her with flaming eyes, she began an hysterical attack of hiccups.

Julia, her voice raised so that she could be heard over Debra's hiccups, calmly replied, "Really Debra, I would have thought that you'd leave your predilections for fun out of polite company." To the shocked amazement of all she continued, "There are some of us who are disgusted by that type of behavior."

Without wasting any time, Phyllis countered, "If we're going to talk about that which disgusts us, then Julia you win the..."

Seeing that Julia's face was turning an unbecoming shade of purple, and hoping to circumvent an apoplectic fit, Susana jumped in, "I'm so sorry everyone, I believe the dessert is completely ruined but no matter, I always have some extra sweet in the kitchen. Moe, would you be a dear and go to the kitchen and ask that the back-up dessert be brought out? Anyone for coffee?"

It was at this point that it occurred to Betty to roar with laughter. Despite her mirth, it was obvious that her face and eyes were taught with nervous tension.

Becoming alarmed, Jack put a hand on Betty's shoulder but as quickly as her laughter had started, it stopped and she resumed her prior morose state.

With a contemptuous look around her, Julia evinced the impression that every person in the room was beneath her dignity.

The friction subsided when Cornelia entered the dining room followed by Moe holding a cake stand with what looked like a seven layer chocolate cake.

Terrorized by Moe's balancing act, Susana rushed to take the cake from him. She beamed at everyone's reaction to the luscious cake.

Jack did his part as host by pouring the dessert wine but before he got to Julia, he walked over to the sideboard and took out a large silver goblet. Standing next to her chair he poured the wine into the goblet saying, "Julia you can't possibly turn down this port. We would take it as an insult considering the limited quantity we have down in the cellar. I've even given you the 'goblet of honor' that is traditionally reserved for the most esteemed guest." And, with a slightly malicious grin, he placed the goblet in front of her.

Fixing a malignant look on her host, Julia said, "So now I'm being strong-armed into depravity! I don't care what this glass is or the fairy tale that goes with it. It still has the devil's own poison in it and your flattery won't get me to drink it." Turning to Cornelia she belligerently continued, "If this extravaganza of a meal is over, please take these tea bags to the kitchen for my tea. That is if you allow that type of beverage here."

Before getting up from the table to do Julia's bidding, Cornelia muttered to Sam and Phyllis, "I don't know who I'd like to murder first, Martha or Julia." As she entered the back hall on her way to the kitchen, she heard the doorbell ringing as if someone had a finger glued to the button. "Julia will just have to wait for her precious cup of tea," she thought to herself and then wondered how long the doorbell had been ringing and who could have such a persistent need to come in. She changed directions and headed towards the front hall.

As she passed the front stairs, she ran smack into Martha who had just turned the corner from the opposite direction.

"Can't a body rest in this 'ouse?" she protested as Cornelia bent down to pick up the hairpins which had escaped from her hair. Looking at Cornelia as if she were the paid help, Martha sniffed, "Even with a broken 'ead I still have to slave round 'ere."

"I'm terribly sorry Martha I was just heading for the kitchen to get a cup of tea for Ms. Peters when I heard all the racket at the door – we couldn't hear the bell in the dining room."

The doorbell continued to ring and Martha looked first at Cornelia and then at the door and then back at Cornelia and expressed, "Well don't just stand there like a brainless chicken, that racket is splittin' my 'ead wide open!"

Cornelia took the hint and meekly walked over to answer the door.

Jim McCarthy stood leaning against the side of the door. "Well it's about time somebody heard my ringing. I was just about to try my luck jumping over the wall!" he said with a wry smile. "I'm sorry I'm late but I got called out on a wild goose chase all the way in the neighboring town."

"Better late than never, but it's I who should apologize. Martha's met with an accident and the party's way out back in the dining room so if it hadn't been for Julia, I would never have known that anyone was at the door."

"Julia's here? I hope you're not serving any liquor!" replied Jim facetiously.

Cornelia laughed, "Oh tons – and she's fit to be tied! Come and join us. We're a little ahead of you but if you don't mind, we'll just sit around while you catch up."

Running a hand over the sleeve of his jacket, Jim replied, "Thanks but if you don't mind, I'd like to clean up."

Cornelia pointed to the door of the guest bathroom, turned to go to the dining room and once again ran into Martha who had been standing directly

45

behind her. "Excuse me Martha, I didn't know you were still here," she apologized.

"Well where else would I be? Ain't it one of my zillion duties to answer this door even when my 'ead's split in two?" wined Martha massaging her head. Cornelia did her best to guide her back to her bedroom.

As Jim McCarthy approached the dining room door he heard Phyllis's voice and then loud laughter from the others. The laughter died abruptly as he entered the room.

"My apologies at being so late but as I was telling Cornelia, some moron called the paper with an urgent story that had me driving all over the district as if on a scavenger hunt. I'd like to get my hands on that person and teach him a thing or two."

"I hope you got a good story after all that," remarked Jack as he poured a glass of wine for Jim.

The newspaperman's attention focused hungrily on the mound of food that Susana had placed in front of him

"What story? I followed what turned out to be a dead end," he said with a mouthful. Then with his glass raised he graciously followed-up, "Cheers, this more than makes up for the wild goose chase."

"Humph. With all the intoxicants, I'm the only person left with clear faculties," snorted Julia glowering at Jim.

"Oh my gosh, I'm sorry Julia," intoned Cornelia jumping from her chair, "I went to order hot water for your tea and then with the confusion of the doorbell and Martha being incapacitated, I guess I got sidetracked. I'll go get your tea right now."

"Sit down, you've been up and down so many times it's making my head spin! I'll go get the tea things," smiled Debra.

"Debra, at least you could have checked that the pot was hot before bringing it to the table," remarked an ungrateful Julia as Debra set down a tray in front of her. Then with a contemptuous grin she continued, "I guess I'm going to have to drink tepid tea or die of thirst." She had no knowledge of the wishful contemplation running through the minds of several in the room.

Having barely spoken during dinner, Betty stood up and said, "Actually I'd love some coffee. I'll be more than happy to bring another pot of hot water," and she walked out of the room returning with a steaming pot that she set in front of Julia.

Jack rose and with a look at his sisters, began, "Now that we've all had the pleasure of each other's company, I think we can get on with the real reason for this gathering. Only a few people besides those of you here know of our intent to donate the parcel of land which abuts this estate with that of the church."

When Jack finished his speech Reverend Peters quietly stammered little words of thanks while the others clapped. His sister sat rigidly with eyes transfixed on her teacup and an amused expression of on her face.

"You know I've hankered after that bit of land for a few years now. It would have been a good business venture for me. But I can't deny that it's a fine gift you're making which will benefit not only the church but the entire village," expressed Sam Taylor as Moe nodded his head in agreement only realizing too late that Julia was staring straight at him with eyes that were boring holes into him.

"Three cheers for the Leslies!" exclaimed Phyllis.

The party all rose as one and with glasses raised toasted the benefactors. No one paid any attention that Julia had remained seated. Her disposition precluded any surprise of her unsocial behavior.

The vicar, thinking that it was beyond rudeness even for Julia to remain seated, walked up to her chair to help her to her feet. But there was no reaction from his sister,

Julia's eyes remained opened with a glassy stare and the disdainful grin had changed to a twisted leer extending from cheek to cheek.

The vicar, with remarkable composure, attempted to gently shake his sister into consciousness but Julia, always contradictory, slid off the chair onto the floor.

The shocked silence was broken by Martha's screams amplified by thunderous lightening followed by the sound of pelting rain against the windows.

Jack and Sam were already moving around the table in an effort to assist the vicar who was kneeling by his sister. Sam took the vicar's elbow and guided him to a nearby chair and asked Debra to look after him. Debra placed an arm around the vicar's shoulders and uttered words of comfort between hiccups.

Susana, distressed that a guest in her home should be taken ill, asked in a high, tremulous voice if she should go and find antacids.

This query had the effect of producing another attack of hysterical laughter from Betty that was subdued after Phyllis stuffed a napkin in her mouth. Recovering she said, "I don't think antacids will do her any good at this point."

"Shouldn't we take her upstairs to lie down

where she'll be more comfortable?" asked Susana ignoring the last comment. When she received no response she continued, "Jack, why don't you and Moe carry Julia up to a guest room. Then as if to herself she added, "Funny, all this time I was under the impression she didn't drink." Coming out of her musing she asked, "Shall I call Dr. Goodman?"

As she went to make the call she muttered to no one in particular, "Poor thing, she just couldn't resist the wine, could she?"

Jack bent down to get a closer look at the motionless body. He made a move as if to touch the body but his arm was grabbed by Jim who said in a low voice, "I believe the customary procedure is to touch nothing and phone for the police."

Chapter 6

"I knew somethin' like this was going to 'appen," Martha hissed while pulling at her hair which was standing on end, "I warned you!"

The next second she was out the door screaming, "Thought I were dead didn't they? I'm not 'angin' 'round so's they can try again! I'm shuttin' myself up in my room!"

"Never a dull moment with her around," murmured Phyllis.

"She's kind of ...hiccup...scary," added Debra.

Horrified by the contorted expression on Julia's face, Moe quickly made for the door holding a handkerchief to his mouth. He stopped when Jim explained that under the circumstances, anyone who left the room would automatically become a person of interest to the police. With a grim expression, Moe was forced to sit at the table as far away from Julia's body as possible.

Having put a call through to the police station, Jack came back to tell the assembled group that Major Geoffrey Sandowne, the Chief Constable of the county had elected to call in Scotland Yard owing to the unusual circumstances. They could expect someone from that hallowed institution within the half hour. They were also advised that until then no one was to leave the premises.

With that in mind, Cornelia suggested that everyone go to the library and with Jack on one side and Cornelia on the other, they guided the vicar across the main hall in the direction of that room.

Both Jim and Sam stood aside as the others filed out of the dining room at which time they closed the double doors and stood self-consciously looking at each other.

"Isn't it customary in novels to lock the door of the room with the body. Do you mind asking Jack where they keep the key?" asked Sam.

Jim smirked and replied, "In the books I've read, they don't leave the body with anyone who could be considered a suspect."

In the library Reverend Peters was placed on a leather armchair by the fire. He walked with a pronounced stoop and looked, if possible, even frailer. "I can't believe it, Julia was in fine health...she seemed to be actually enjoying the food...didn't once mention anything about not feeling well...", his voice trailed off as he stared into the fire. Susana, Cornelia and Debra sat around him trying to comfort him.

"It must have been something very sudden – a coronary or possibly a hemorrhage," volunteered Cornelia kindly.

After a few moments, the vicar, still gazing at the flames, replied with a far off voice, "Yes, yes, of course something like that."

"That's right, Cornelia," spoke Susana, "It must have been a heart attack or something of that nature. I don't see why the police have been called in. Couldn't Dr. Goodman examine Julia?" Then realizing the gravity of the situation, Susana jumped up and ran from the room calling for someone to find

Dr. Goodman.

From the doorway, Susana beckoned her sister. "Cornelia, I know Julia is…" then casting a glance at the vicar, she lowered her voice to a stage whisper and continued, "…under the weather. But I still don't understand why the police have to come to tell us what we already know. A doctor is the one who has to sign the de---, um…the papers. Isn't he?"

Jack and Phyllis stood by the small art deco bar drinking bourbon and talking quietly. Betty sat in a corner and watched.

"I didn't care for the old cat but she looked pretty ghastly lying in that position with her gaping eyes and horrid grin. She must have had a massive stroke. In a way, she's pretty lucky to go like that," opined Phyllis.

With a slight grimace Jack replied, "Yeah, but how do we know she didn't suffer? That look on her face wasn't too pleasant."

At that moment there were footsteps heard in the hallway and almost immediately the library door opened. Two men in plain clothes entered the room followed by a constable who remained standing by the door.

Dr. Goodman entered the room in a professional capacity so his deportment was studied and professional. He replied to the greetings from the various persons in the room but it was obvious that he was not there to socialize. He was of average height with the typical male baldness pattern however his devotion to bicycling had the effect of making him look younger than his actual sixty years. Having lived and practiced medicine in the village for most of thirty years, he enjoyed being thought of as a country doctor and maintained his medical office in a little bungalow next door to his home which was conveniently located on one of the little side streets leading off the village green. Being the only medical man in the village he was an important member of the community. His no nonsense manner in dealing with patients, many of whom he had brought into the world, was a mixture of strict orders sprinkled with kindness – a mix which made him one of the best liked and trusted individuals in the village. It was widely acknowledged that his razor sharp intellect along with his keen sense of humor and wit were formidable tools at his disposal. His busy practice left him very little spare time for himself, but whenever his wife and grown children brought up the subject of retirement, he would insist that his hearing was declining, a signal to his family that any further discussion would be futile.

Taking off his hat and coat and dropping them onto an empty chair he addressed the Leslies, "I declined your kind invitation for tonight because of a meeting of county coroners down at the Epping police station and low and behold I receive your message from my exchange. Funny how medicine works," he said somewhat obtusely.

Turning to the vicar he continued in a sympathetic tone, "I came as soon as I got word I apologize for the delay." Looking at the rest of the party he continued, "Providentially, Major Sandowne and officers from the Scotland Yard CID were meeting at the police station tonight. He asked them to accompany me and they have graciously consented. I'd like you to meet Chief Detective Inspector Alistair Bunson, and, of course, you all know Detective Sergeant Mike Rogers who'll be along presently."

If one didn't know that Inspector Bunson held the lauded title of Chief Inspector, CID, New Scotland Yard, one would never have guessed it. His short stature and slight build had nearly cost him entrance to the police academy and even now at the mellow age of 56 he still battled with his slight frame and was famous amongst his colleagues for his predilection for antacids. Inspector Bunson's quiet, nervous demeanor gave the impression that he operated in unknown waters and had difficulty determining how to navigate. In truth, his slow and methodical technique had proved successful in many difficult cases and won him praise and promotion. His deportment was shy, almost timid and his graying mustache had a habit of twitching when he was either thinking or angry. Hence, the nickname of "Bunny" which no one uttered within range of the Inspector's hearing.

"I suppose you'd like to see the body?" asked Jack once the formal introductions had been made.

"Well, I'd pre..." Inspector Bunson started to reply but was interrupted by Susana who leapt in front of him.

"Oh, Inspector, so kind of you to come all this way at this hour and in this dreadful storm but I really don't think we'll be needing the police. One of our guests," Susana struggled for the right words, "she must have had a stroke or hemorrhage or something sudden like that. Dreadful - isn't it?"

Chief Inspector Bunson listened to Susana and tried to hide the mixture of skepticism and surprise on his face.

When she had finished, he replied, "Thank you, Mrs. er..."

Susana stepped in, "Leslie, Inspector. My

sister and I continue the tradition of using our maiden names at Blandings – much easier for the locals."

Not quite comprehending, the inspector continued, "Yes...thank you. I'm sure Dr. Goodman will be able to give us a more detailed idea of the cause of death. If you don't mind, I will accompany him when he examines the body," and he followed Jack and Dr. Goodman to the door.

Reassured Susana, in an about face said, "There now, no worries. This inspector seems like such a nice man. Doesn't seem like a policeman at all. Does he?" and resumed her seat nearest the vicar.

Chief Inspector Bunson stopped halfway to the door and gave a slightly self-conscious cough then turned and said, "Constable Dibbs will be taking information from each of you. For your protection I've placed constables outside the premises. We're very grateful for your cooperation and of course you will be allowed to return to your homes once the constable has your informal statements."

Susana smiled, "Ohh, it will be nice to see Mikey! And to think he's working for Scotland Yard – no one would have believed it knowing him as a boy." Then more to herself than anyone she murmured, "I wonder why we need protection?"

"So we sit here trapped like canaries." Announced Betty, who sat in a corner half hidden by the smoke from her cigarettes.

Chapter 7

"Why Betty dear, no one said anything about being 'trapped'. I'm sure we can go as we please - can't we?" replied Susana looking around the room for validation.

"Aside from the fact that we've just been warned that the police are guarding all the exits, we still have to be interviewed by Constable Dibbs," said Sam as he rose to join Phyllis at the bar.

"Can I mix everyone a drink?" asked Phyllis to the room, "It looks like it's going to be a long evening."

"I guess I'll have my...hiccup...usual, and I wouldn't...hiccup...mind if you made it a double," replied Debra.

Trying to keep his voice from cracking, Moe the 'Ways and Means Committee' member said, "My goodness, it's been an unusual evening. We...I...have some business to attend to so I'll just say goodnight."

"Yes, it certainly has been unusual. I hope you've enjoyed yourself - I mean I hope you've enjoyed the food, that is, oh dear, it's been so chaotic I can't think straight," said Susana looking around with an anxious expression and added, "You don't look so well, are you alright?"

Moe was already at the door and turned

stammering, "Oh...yes. I...hope so."

As he walked out into the hall his movement was abruptly hampered by Detective Sergeant Michael Rogers, a young officer recently promoted to Scotland Yard CID and who coincidentally was a born and bred native of Epping. He had been an accomplished police cadet, eager and intelligent with an uncanny ability to get to the core of a problem and find the solution quickly. He became a favorite of both his fellow cadets and his instructors facilitating his movement up the ranks. The fact that this particular homicide investigation would take place amongst people whom he had known all his life was daunting and weighed heavily on his mind.

Nervously straightening his tie, Moe greeted the Sergeant like an old friend and stammered his apologies. "So sorry...dreadfully hot...in there."

Sergeant Rogers did not move. Squaring his wide shoulders and to his surprise, found himself repeating the exact lines uttered by detectives in films, "I'm sorry Mr. Stone but you can't leave this room. I've been ordered to stay with Constable Dibbs and help take down any information in regards the evening's events."

The village of Epping, much to its credit, had never been a hot bed of criminal activity. Aside from the usual deaths from illness and old age, a couple of accidental drownings and a suicide fifty years previously, a death by homicide was an anomaly.

Moe was not happy at not being allowed to leave and he took on a blustery attitude in the hopes of intimidating the young officer.

Unfortunately for him, Officer Rogers had a one-track mind. Spreading his arms out he walked forward making it difficult for the other man to continue his progress. "We have been ordered not to allow anyone out of this room. Please return to it immediately."

It was a strongly held belief by a majority of the senior officers at the Yard that Rogers' powers of persuasion were a combination of his very creative, to put it mildly, problem solving skills aided by his wholesome good looks.

By this time the door of the library was bulging with all its occupants trying to see and hear the goings on in the hall.

Without physical contact, Officer Rogers propelled Moe into the room as the staring occupants quickly retreated inside. Trying to maintain a professional decorum yet unable to ignore the fact that he had close ties with the majority of the people in the room, Officer Rogers nodded his head in greeting then assumed the role of an officer of Scotland Yard and proceeded with his official duties.

Meanwhile, Sam Taylor and Jim McCarthy sat on the floor guarding the dining room door. With the approach of the inspector and doctor, they both got up and sheepishly began dusting themselves off.

"You boys playing marbles?" asked Dr. Goodman before introducing the Inspector.

"No I'm afraid neither one of us wanted to leave the room until the police arrived," spoke Sam handing over the key.

"Makes my job a lot easier, thank you," said the Inspector as he and the doctor stepped into the dining room.

The farmer and newspaperman, both eager for information, followed them inside. The inspector stopped in his tracks so that Jim stumbled into him.

Heedless of Jim's apologies, the inspector,

hands in his pockets and nose twitching, stood just inside the room taking in his surroundings.

"I guess we should get out of the way," said Sam conscious of the fact that the authorities were now in command and with the knowledge that police investigations are seldom conducted in front of spectators.

"Hmm? No, you don't have to leave unless you don't like looking at dead bodies," replied the Inspector absentmindedly.

Before Sam had a chance to answer, he was pushed aside by the forensic team of photographers, fingerprint, and DNA experts who, after receiving instructions from Inspector Bunson began their assorted tasks. The Inspector opened a French door leading to the back garden and poking his head out called to a constable who had been standing outside. Sam and Jim with morbid curiosity, attempted to follow the activity but were stopped in their tracks by the constable who motioned them to remain where they were.

When the photographer had finished photographing the body, it was Dr. Goodman's turn. After carefully examining the body, which had come to rest on its side after slipping from the chair, Dr. Goodman turned the body onto its back. He looked up at the Inspector who nodded to him in silent communication.

"I don't see any contusions or trauma anywhere on the body," said Dr. Goodman getting up. "We'll do the postmortem tonight and I'll have the results in the morning."

Inspector Bunson called to the head of the forensic team and spoke to him quietly. Then politely asked Sam and Jim to accompany him and Dr.

Goodman to the library to join the other guests. Dr. Goodman stopped at the library door and said, "I'll be pushing off, Alistair. It's going to be a long night and I'd like to get started. I'll be in touch." And so saying he continued along the hallway towards the front door.

The constable stationed at the library door quickly opened the door for the Scotland Yard men. The occupants of the library, while trying to maintain their composure and social grace, all had a common thought that immediately surfaced upon hearing the library door open. As if one, they stopped their conversations and with questioning looks of alarm written on their faces, turned to stare at the inspector.

The vicar was the first to speak and in a barely audible voice said, "I suppose it was a sudden heart attack, Inspector?"

It was obvious to the others that this question had taken great effort on the part of its speaker. It never ceased to amaze the Inspector when death came suddenly to a loved one, the family automatically assumed a heart or cerebral problem. He had decided long ago that this was a form of unconscious solace.

Susana's instinctive desire to comfort the vicar precipitated her to say, "Thomas, of course it was a heart attack! Wasn't Julia fine one minute and under the table the next?"

Choking on her drink, Phyllis whispered to Jack, "Ohhh, that was an unconscious slip of the tongue, even for Susana."

Jack, aware that the others were making a deliberate attempt to avoid looking at anyone, asked, "Inspector, is this party going to be an all-nighter or are we going to get to go to our own beds soon?"

Inspector Bunson had been standing quietly

inside the door. His startled response gave the impression that he too longed for the comfort of his own bed and it took him a few seconds to respond. Automatically putting a hand in his coat pocket for his antacids, he gave a slight cough and said, "The procedure in circumstances of this kind is to get preliminary information from any witnesses. I have been told this has already been done. Within the next twenty four hours we will be in touch with everyone to get your formal statements." He finished with another self-conscious cough.

From behind him, Sam asked, "To what 'circumstances' are you referring Inspector?" This query had the effect of loosening everyone's tongue and once again they all began to speak at the same time.

Cornelia, distressed at the thought of having to sit in a drafty room all night said with feeling, "Yes, Inspector, it seems perfectly straightforward that Julia suffered a coronary and that's all there is to it."

Jim added, "We were all in the room together Inspector, I'm sure that if anyone of us had seen something unusual we would have mentioned it."

Phyllis volunteered that she and Debra had made arrangements to go hiking early the next morning and would appreciate knowing when they would be allowed to go home.

Betty sat speechless, eyes staring at the other guests and unconsciously clasping and unclasping her hands.

"Inspector, I hope you can see the predicament I'm in. As a newspaperman I'd like to get this story in print ASAP," added Jim.

"Yeah, it'd be quite a laugh if some other paper scooped you on this one! You'd never live it down at the Ravens Roost!" snickered Moe.

Inspector Bunson, patiently waiting for everyone to voice their opinion, thanked them for their cooperation and told them they were free to leave. There was an immediate group sigh of relief as the guests assembled themselves in preparation to leave.

Officer Rogers thanked the departing guests for their cooperation and bid them goodnight while the Inspector, no longer the main attraction, stood against a sofa quietly observing each individual. Before the first person left the room, he cleared his throat and in a deferential tone said, "Please remember that we will be contacting you to take your formal statements and if it wouldn't be too much trouble, we'd like to ask that for the next few days you stay in town and if you need to travel it would be appreciated if you would let us know."

In turn, the assembled guests who were jostling for the door, turned questioning faces in the direction of Inspector Bunson but eager to make their escape, quickly filed out of the library without a word.

Chapter 8

It was almost one thirty in the morning when the last guest had left and Betty had gone upstairs to her room.

Jack headed for the bar while Cornelia and Susana dropped into chairs. Officer Rogers continued to log in information while the Inspector looked over his shoulder.

"Inspector, would you or Sergeant Rogers like something to drink?" enquired Jack.

Sergeant Rogers looked up expectantly but hearing his superior's refusal, replied, "No, thank you, sir."

"Well then Inspector, obviously there must be something suspicious about Julia's death or you and your men wouldn't still be roaming around. Not to mention that you did sound rather ominous what with your warnings, " observed Cornelia. "What exactly is happening here Inspector? I feel it is our right to be informed if Julia's death was due to something other than natural causes."

"Oh Cornelia, don't be ridiculous, you said yourself earlier that Julia died of a coronary. Are you changing your mind now?" asked a bewildered and slightly flustered Susana.

"I apologize for any undue distress but it is impossible for me to give you any more information until Dr. Goodman has presented the formal autopsy report," replied the Inspector. Seeing Susana's look of concern he added, "I expect we'll have it in a few hours."

In response to a knock at the library door, Sergeant Rogers opened the door and was heard speaking with someone in low tones. When he was finished, he closed the door and walked to the Inspector and another conversation ensued.

Making no pretense of their intent to get any snippet of information, Susana and Cornelia sat on the edge of their seats heads cocked in the direction of the officers.

When he had finished speaking with Sergeant Rogers, the Inspector approached the siblings saying, "Once again I must apologize for our intrusion into your home. I have just been informed that my people are finished in both the kitchen and the dining room. So there will be..."

"Your people in my kitchen?" echoed Susana standing up, "What people and what were they doing in my kitchen?"

Inspector Bunson turned blood shot eyes at Susana and said, "Please don't be upset Mrs. Leslie. We have just borrowed the cooking implements along with the china and crystal that were used tonight. Everything was carefully wrapped and will be returned to you in pristine condition. We have a receipt of the items here for you."

"I don't understand Inspector. Do you Cornelia?" Susana turned fretfully to Cornelia who was staring open mouthed at the Inspector.

Jack went up to Susana and putting an arm

around her said, "I think what the inspector is trying to tell us is that something in the food we served might have made Julia ill."

Looking at Jack and rolling her eyes, Cornelia uttered, "Now you've done it."

The floodgates had been opened. Susana began to wring her hands, whine and sob all at the same time. "Never, ever in all my time cooking has anyone ever been remotely sick. How can you say that? It's just too horrible to imagine! Can't you do something?" she implored wringing her hands in desperation.

Inspector Bunson, looking decidedly uncomfortable, begged to be excused and bidding them all a good night, headed out the door with his Sergeant immediately behind him.

A few seconds after the door had closed, Sergeant Rogers popped his head back into the room to remind the siblings that he and the Inspector would be returning in the morning.

Linking her arm through Susana's, Cornelia said, "C'mon Susana, we need to get some rest. It's been a long day and an even longer night. I'm going to make us some hot Ovaltine to take up to our rooms."

"Never mind the Ovaltine girls, I'll take up a hot toddy," replied their brother making a face.

Cornelia and Susana made their way to the kitchen where they heard the din of what sounded like someone rummaging through a utensil drawer.

"I don't know that I feel up to having anything to eat or drink Cornelia. My head is aching with everything that's happened tonight - Martha what are you doing with that bag?" asked a teary Susana.

Without looking up Martha responded, "It's all over the village that 'er dyin' weren't no accident and I don't know about you but I ain't gonna be 'acked to death by some psycho so I'm takin' the knives for protection."

In an effort to understand, Cornelia said, "Martha, you're *supposed* to be in bed nursing your head and how do you know what everyone in the village thinks?"

Martha looked up and with an impatient toss of her head said, "That wicked old prune's dead, ain't she? And the police were 'ere weren't they? And Dr. Goodman's gonna cut 'er open ain't 'e? O'course everyone's gonna know that there's a 'omicidal maniac on the loose. And don't think I'm gonna spend another night in this 'ouse of 'orrrors!"

It had been a long time since Martha's antics had astounded anyone in the Leslie household and tonight was no exception. With knowing looks the sisters left Martha to carry on her looting in private.

"How much do you want to bet she's going to give another one of her phony notices?" sighed Susana as they climbed the stairs.

"Who cares? She's forever moaning and groaning with hysterics. I know she's not all there but I'm getting fed up with her high drama and I for one will be happy to see the back of her," replied Cornelia leaving Susana at the door of her room. "I'm almost too tired to change into pajamas. See you in a few minutes – if I don't collapse at the bathroom sink that is."

Ever since their childhood, it had been a ritual for the sisters to drink mugs of hot Ovaltine in Susana's bedroom when something troubled one or the other.

Wearing a quilted pink satin bed jacket, Susana got into her bed piled high with blankets and a thick down comforter. When she was comfortably situated with her mug of Ovaltine on her lap, she looked around her and wondered how in this safest of all places something so horrible could have taken place. Just as she was making herself more and more agitated with thoughts of blood and knives, Cornelia walked in wearing a flowing robe.

"Cornelia, do you think there's a homicidal maniac loose in the village?" asked her sister tremulously.

"Of course not, you should know by now how the village people like to spread rumors and gossip! Every time a story gets told it gets more and more fantastic," reassured Cornelia trying to sound like she believed what she was saying.

"Well what about the part that Julia's death wasn't an accident?" blinked Susana making a loud gulping noise as she swallowed her milk.

"Oh don't let that upset you. We know everyone who was here tonight. Do you think any of them had plans to do away with Julia?" Having said this Cornelia became aware of a faint warning signal coming from a little corner of her brain but she was too tired to try to wrestle it out.

At eight o'clock in the morning, Cornelia walked out of her room dressed and anxiously contemplating the interview with the police. She was startled to see that her sister also fully dressed was going down the stairs ahead of her.

"Couldn't you sleep?" she asked Susana.

"Well if Martha has really left I thought I'd make breakfast for us and I'm sure the Inspector and

Mikey will want something when they get here," answered her sister.

Cornelia was surprised at Susana's matter of fact attitude. She had expected her to be still perseverating over the events of the night before.

"What's *your* reason for being up at this hour? Couldn't *you* sleep?" enquired Susana.

"Can't complain. I just wanted to be up when Mikey and the Inspector arrived," answered Cornelia trying to sound as if it was a long lost relative they were expecting.

As they came down the stairs, the familiar aroma of burnt food and coffee assailed their nostrils.

"That woman will never learn how to boil water," expressed Susana in a resigned voice. Then with a frown continued, "Oh, oh, I guess that means she hasn't left doesn't it?

"And why should we be so lucky?" replied her sister shaking her head.

Upon entering the kitchen, they found Martha with her back to them standing in front of the stove madly stirring a pot. At the sound of their footsteps she screamed and picked up the nearest object that just happened to be a butcher knife.

"Ugh, it's only you two," she said in disgust, "I was 'opin' it was the 'omicidal maniac 'cause now I'm prepared." She wielded the knife as if she had just graduated from a ninja academy.

Resigned to Martha's strange antics, Susana calmly walked over to the coffeemaker, and without saying a word lifted the pot and dumped its contents into the sink. After some scrubbing, she proceeded to brew a new pot of coffee.

As she poured the steaming coffee into three mugs, she said lightly, "I'm so glad you decided against leaving us Martha. We know you didn't mean what you said. Did you?"

"And I thought we were rid of the village nosey parker," sniffed the housekeeper looking up from her stirring. "But if you must know, I'm 'ere this mornin' 'cause my cousin Billy's in charge of the inpestigation and 'e told me that I'm safer 'ere than anywhere else 'cause a killer never goes back to the scene of the crime." She gave the sisters a meaningful look.

An incredulous Cornelia choked on her coffee and after Susana had stopped whacking her on the back was able to ask, "You mean that Inspector Bunson has turned over the case to your cousin?"

Martha rolled her eyes and sighed, conveying her thoughts of the sisters' I.Q., "Yep, and if you don't believe me, Billy's outside the kitchen door right now," she stated with pride.

Both sisters got up and rushed to the door. Constable Jenkins was standing just outside the kitchen door, albeit not too comfortably due to the weight he carried and the uniform that was just a wee bit constricting around his mid section. On seeing the Leslie sisters he tugged at his uniform jacket in an unsuccessful effort to cover a significant gut, while at the same time making a clumsy salute.

Billy Jenkins was indeed one of only a handful of Epping constables. Details of how he was able to join the ranks were sketchy, and were a good source of conjecture at the Raven's Roost. Some held that it was owing to the Jenkins family being one of the oldest families in Epping, having settled in the area as far back as the sixteen hundred's surviving by their wits and then just barely. The family was famed for its prodigious reproduction of dimwitted individuals and the residents of the village considered themselves the guardians and protectors of this most eccentric family.

Throwing family loyalty out the window, Martha yelled, "That'll be his sixth cup of coffee this mornin'. And don't go askin' 'im if 'e wants any more to eat neither. 'E's already eatin'all the bacon and I'm 'avin' a dickens of a time tryin' to divide the two eggs 'e didn't wolf down between all you people."

"That explains the mad stirring," whispered Cornelia to no one in particular.

"What was that you said?" asked Martha looking at Cornelia through squinty eyes.

Cornelia thought quickly and said, "Oh nothing, Scotland Yard probably thinks Constable Jenkins the best man to assist them due to the high security precautions involved in investigations of this type."

"Yep, 'e told me, in confidence, that this 'ouse is officially under surveillance." replied Martha hoping this arrow would find its mark.

Cornelia cast a meaningful glance at her sister and said, "I think it's time we left Martha to get on with her busy schedule."

Taking the hint, Susana hastily replied, "Oh...er...yes, of course. Martha we don't want to get in your way. Especially when you're preparing a meal." Turning to look back she added, "You can stop your ministrations on those poor eggs. I believe only Jack and Betty will be at breakfast. Is that a piece of egg shell in your hair?"

The two sisters had just stepped into the front hall when the doorbell rang announcing the arrival of Inspector Bunson and Officer Rogers.

Coming to a sudden halt Susana worriedly asked, "Before we open the door shouldn't we practice what we're going to say?"

"Whatever for? Is there something you've not told us? Should we be worried that you might come after us with Martha's butcher knife?" laughed Cornelia. In a more serious tone she said, "We have nothing to hide and I'm sure the inspector is aware of the fact that we had nothing to do with Julia's death."

"Don't you know why he's come to interview us? It's because he suspects that we, that is, I served tainted food! Have you ever been inside of a jail before?" asked Susana on the verge of tears.

"Don't get worked up or you'll definitely make the Inspector suspicious," responded Cornelia adding to herself, "Anyone who could possibly imagine you in the role of a murderer is a complete imbecile."

On opening the front door and after the greetings were over, Susana could not resist asking Inspector Bunson if he was going to arrest her.

Picturing himself at Scotland Yard with a handcuffed Susana on a charge of homicide while his colleagues looked on was a thought too mortifying to contemplate and the inspector cringed in horror. Wiping his brow he tried to smile reassuringly and said, "No need to worry Mrs. Leslie. Really, just routine in homicide cases." As he finished the sentence, he knew by Susana's expression that he had used an unfortunate choice of words.

Forgetting her usual attention to social custom, Susana remained glued to the spot and while unconsciously blocking entry into the house she asked in a stunned voice, "Homicide! But that means that someone purposely killed Julia!" Turning sheet white, she whispered, "And in our home. What are we going to do?"

Inspector Bunson, looking embarrassed at having made such a blunder, looked to his Sergeant in an appeal for help.

Aware that his senior officer had committed a gaffe and was suffering quietly, Sergeant Rogers was quick to respond. "Actually what the Inspector meant to say, M'am is that the postmortem has been concluded and the official ruling on the cause of death is suspicious or in other terms, not due to natural causes." Seeing that Susana's expression continued to be one of horror, the Chief Inspector continued, "You can rest assured that there was nothing wrong with any food that was served."

Cornelia, aware that the situation could quickly nosedive, joined in, saying, "You see! We already knew that Julia's death was unexpected, and you just hear Mike saying that there was nothing wrong with the food we served. So we have nothing to worry about."

Inspector Bunson felt it was now safe to proceed, "If we could just move to the library we'd like to go over the events of last night."

"Ah, the officials have arrived to administer the third degree," quipped Jack as he came down the front stairs.

"Good morning gentlemen, care to join me in some breakfast?"

"Breakfast will have to wait because the Inspector wants us in the library - are you very hungry?" asked Susana pulling him by the arm.

"I apologize but we must follow protocol…rules you know," replied Inspector Bunson ineffectually.

73

"Please don't let your breakfast get cold. We intend to interview the Mrs. Leslies first. I will let you know when the Inspector is ready for you," added the Sergeant.

As Jack approached the kitchen, he heard Martha speaking to someone.

"E're I am, slavin' away in front of this 'ot stove since the crack of dawn and you just waltz in and all you want is a cuppa tea? Don't 'ave no manners."

"Morning Martha, what's cookin?" greeted Jack planting a kiss on Martha's cheek resulting in girlish giggles. Taking the chair next to Betty and moving it as close as possible to hers, he continued, "I'm starving. Nothing like being sloshed to give me a good appetite!"

"At least there's one person in this 'ere 'ouse what's not flippin' bonkers," said Martha setting a platter piled high with rubbery eggs, burnt sausages, half cooked bacon and cold potatoes in front of Jack. Looking at him through her white eyelashes, she continued coyly, "My cousin Billy, what's standin' outside the door, tried to eat everythin' in site this mornin' but I saved these special for you Mr. Jack." Then jumping as if she had stepped on hot coals, she ran to the stove, picked up a pan and bringing it to the table, said, "Stavers, I darn'd almost forgot to give you yur fried bread. Ain't no breakfast without fried bread."

"Mmm, made with real bacon drippings, yummy," said Jack looking at the charred piece of bread and wondering, not for the first time, at the Jenkins family constitution.

Betty looked away in disgust and sipped her tea. When Martha's back was turned, Jack spoke to

Betty in low tones, "I'm sorry I didn't hear you get up or I would have taken you out to breakfast – we can still go out after I make a pretense of eating." In normal tones he continued, "By the way, how long have you been down here?"

"She strolled in just a couple of minutes a'fore ya," put in Martha.

Betty gave her a withering look but continued sipping her tea without saying a word.

"How come we didn't see you come down? We were all standing in the front hall talking to the Inspector and Mike," asked Jack.

"I took the back stairs so I could avoid your sisters," answered Betty, unaware of Martha's gaping mouth.

Chapter 9

In the library, the sisters sat close together on the sofa across from the Inspector while Sergeant Rogers sat at a table with his laptop.

"It's not as damp out this morning," began the Inspector.

"No," replied the sisters in unison smiling nervously.

The Inspector continued, "I believe the weather will hold for the next couple of days."

"I hope so, our fall roses will mildew if the dampness persists," replied Cornelia.

There was an embarrassing lull in the conversation until Susana contemplated, "Well at least the ground won't be frozen for Julia's funeral. Will it?"

Mindful that any semblance of being in command of the situation had eroded, the Inspector cleared his throat and asked, "Would you ladies mind giving us a timeline of the activities of last night?"

"Oh yes Inspector," began Susana hardly waiting for him to finish, "I sat up all night thinking about it and I've come to the conclusion that Julia's death was either a coronary or an accidental suicide."

A sharp ping was heard coming from the

direction of Sergeant Rogers' computer while it's red-faced user studiously stared at the screen.

With self-control worthy of the Victoria Cross the Inspector managed a wan smile and said, "Thank you, Mrs. Leslie that's certainly something we will have to investigate. Can you tell us why you think Ms. Peters might have accidentally killed herself?"

"Certainly Inspector. I can't tell you how many times I caught her staring at me with a murderous look in her eyes. I wouldn't be surprised if she had meant to do away...oh dear, I suddenly don't feel too well...be right back... excuse me?" Susana quickly left the room, leaving the others in a stupefied silence.

Cornelia was the first to recover and in an heroic effort to gloss over her sister's latest blooper said, "Well Inspector, I'm sure I can give you the information you need as far as the timeline goes. My sister was running back and forth between the kitchen, solarium and dining room attending to the meal preparation that I'm sure she really didn't have time to pay attention to anything else. So you see, it's really not necessary that she be present."

Next on the detectives' list was Jack Leslie. It didn't take long for Sergeant Rogers to find him sitting on the last step of the stairs reading the morning newspaper.

"Someone finally took matters into their own hands. Funny it took this long," he said as they headed to the library where he sat casually with one leg over the arm of a chair.

"I'm afraid I won't be much help Inspector," he said lightly, "I'm embarrassed to say that I spent most of the evening and well into the early morning in a complete fog of alcohol. And now I'm swimming in coffee and feeling non too well – Martha's cooking you know."

Jack's casual, care-free behavior made the Inspector's nose twitch. He wasn't sure whether to take his off-hand remarks at face value or as affectations and it annoyed him that he could not decide on the right tactic to use. He finally settled on the safe, if not always successful, stoic, professional cop attitude. Casually fingering a paperweight, the inspector replied, "Understood. But to the best of your recollection, does anything stand out in your mind as being unusual?"

"You mean aside from seeing Julia dead on the floor of the dining room?" grinned Jack. "Inspector, you can't tell me that you haven't noticed that with two sisters like Cornelia and Susana, not to mention the odd characters with which they surround themselves, that anything could possibly be considered as normal in this house!"

The door of the library suddenly opened and Betty entered the room, "Oh, Inspector, I'd completely forgotten that you were going to be here this morning," she lied, "But since I'm here would you mind if I stayed?" Not waiting for his answer, she proceeded to make herself comfortable on the sofa.

After a slight cough the Inspector smiled and said, "Certainly, Ms. Smith. We're just gathering some preliminary information. I was just asking Mr. Leslie if he saw anything or anyone acting out of the ordinary last night."

Picking up a magazine and casually flipping through the pages, Betty mumbled, "That's an easy one. Everyone around here is completely bonkers!"

"Betty's quite new to Epping, Inspector. She's

not used to the intricacies or the eccentricities which make up our charming English village," volunteered Jack.

"I see," replied the Inspector unconvinced. "Well then can you tell us where you lived prior to coming to Epping and how long you've been here?"

Betty looked at the inspector for a few seconds before replying and then getting up from the sofa, walked towards the French windows and said, "Certainly Inspector. I applied for the temporary teaching position at the elementary school six months ago. I thought at the time, that the country air would be a nice change from the rat race in London – boy was I wrong."

Inspector Bunson stood quietly contemplating why he had to try to elicit coherent responses from a blonde dingbat while his officer sat quietly enjoying himself.

"Well, on the evening of the death of Ms. Peters, was there anyone or anything which might have caught your attention as being odd, that is to say, out of the ordinary?"

Betty turned from the window and with an impatient tug at the curtain said, "I told you, Inspector, nothing about anything or anyone in this village surprises me."

The last person to be interviewed at the manor was Martha Jenkins. This was a conscious decision on the part of the Inspector. He knew that it was his duty to interview all persons who had had contact with the deceased however he suspected that anything Martha had to say would only cause him indigestion coupled with a severe headache.

The two detectives made their way to the kitchen where Martha was in her usual chaotic state attempting to prepare lunch.

As they entered, she managed to stop her frenzied ministrations and quipped, "So you finally saw fit to come to me, aye?"

Inspector Bunson trying his best to stay calm, took such a long deep breath that Officer Rogers wondered if he were going to pass out.

Martha squinted at the inspector and then said to Officer Rogers, "Betcha 'e never was one of them 'ealthy kids - probably always sick and 'avin' to stay 'ome."

"I am here in an official capacity Martha and I'd appreciate your cooperation," replied Inspector Bunson swallowing a handful of antacids. "Now tell us what you were doing on the night of Julia Peters' death."

Martha threw her washcloth on the floor and with her hands on her hips, walked over to stand in front of the Inspector's chair. In a mocking tone she replied, "Whadya' think I was doin'? A kitchen full of pansy, show-off cooks, makin' a mess everywhere, askin' me to fetch this and fetch that - I 'ad my 'ands full just tryin' to stay away from 'em. Not to mention I 'ad to 'ave one ear cocked listenin' for the front door."

Turning to speak to Mike Rogers, she continued, "We used to make fun of the brainy ones like 'im. I'd like to know why Billy ain't runnin' this show? 'E'd find the person who threw me down the cellar, without askin' these gosh darn stupid questions."

Inspector Bunson once again looked as if he would have an apoplectic fit. "Martha, if you don't cooperate and give us direct answers to our questions I'm going to have to lock you up in the police station."

"Alright with me, Mr. Smarty Pants, probably be safer in there than out 'ere with you tryin' to find the mad killer."

Sergeant Rogers decided it was high time he took over the one-sided interview. "Martha, I've told the Inspector how clever you are with your second-sight. Do you think that could have been why you were targeted?" he asked charmingly, trying his best to placate her as the Inspector rolled his eyes heavenward and took out his bottle of tablets.

Martha lowered her eyes and giggled holding her apron to her face. Then in almost the same second she became serious and said, "I warned them, I knew there was trouble brewin'."

Officer Rogers nodded in agreement and prompted, "Can you tell us what kind of trouble?"

"You want to know what kind of trouble? If you only knew..." Martha stared in front of her with glazed over eyes.

It was no use trying to get Martha to explain as she remained transfixed and unresponsive.

A steady drizzle had drenched the village of Epping during the night but by early morning the countryside was bathed in a watery sunshine.

Epping Town Hall was selected as the site for the inquest. Well before the stated hour of nine o'clock, the curious villagers had gathered on the green in front of the old building. The coroner, an elderly retired lawyer sat before a packed room and in no uncertain terms outlined how he expected the proceedings to be handled. His final words directed at the gallery exemplified his strict attitude, "I'm warning you that if there's one spoken word from the audience - and I mean all you men standing in the back - I'll have the officer of the court escort you out."

All those present at the dinner party were briefly questioned. Susana's anxious deportment and sometimes contradictory answers caused the coroner on several occasions to stop to look at his notes in order to recall the original question. In the end, she had unwittingly succeeded in portraying herself as the prime suspect.

Martha, dressed in her favorite assortment of ill-fitting clothes held reign amongst the towns people. Her evidence which was more opinion than fact indiscriminately implicated everyone in the room whether at the party or not, drawing several loud gasps from those in attendance.

The inquest was finally adjourned with the finding of death due to ingestion of poison or poisons unknown. This decree would facilitate the continuation of the Scotland Yard investigation. It was also announced that the funeral of Julia Peters would take place in two days' time.

Cornelia and Susana who were seated on either side of the Vicar during the proceeding kindly persuaded him to have lunch at the "Buns and Tarts" the village tea shop which also served a palatable lunch.

The Vicar's already fragile state was now even more tenuous since his sister's death and Cornelia and Susana fussed over him.

"Oh look," said Susana chattily, making her way to a table by the window. "My favorite table - so much sunlight. Don't you agree?"

"Not to mention you get to see everything that

goes on along the Main Street," quipped Cornelia as they sat down.

The entry of the main mourner along with the owners of the residence where the suspicious death had occurred caused quite a stir in the kitchen of the Buns and Tarts. Nora, the owner of the establishment, her arms elbow deep in flour, heard her two young servers, Ginny and Liz bickering over who was going to take the order. Giving them a quick scolding, she wiped her hands on her apron and went to the table herself while the two girls huddled behind the pastry case staring in ghoulish delight.

"Julia enjoyed this place, especially their cream teas," said the Vicar looking around at the tiny but exquisitely clean shop. "I preferred having my tea at the vicarage by a toasty fire. But Julia needed to be in the center of the comings and goings of Epping. She was very involved in village life as you well know," he smiled remembering.

This was a perfect opening for Cornelia, "Yes, the Women's Institute won't be the same without Julia. I don't know who we'll get to replace her."

"That's right," joined in Susana. "I mean president of the Women's Institute for ten years! Why I don't remember any past president who had more than a two year term!" Then furrowing her brows, she continued, "She wouldn't give anyone a chance. Would she?"

Aware of her sister's slip, and the funny smile on the vicar's face Cornelia hastily added, "Not that anyone else could do a better job."

"I know what you mean, Susana. Julia liked everything done her way. She was like that at home too," replied Reverend Peters graciously. "We had a dickens of a time keeping help at the vicarage. They never stayed for more than a couple of months."

Chapter 10

Coming out of the inquest, Inspector Bunson was not a happy man. He spoke to Officer Rogers who followed at his side, "I received a call from the Chief Constable this morning. He's pushing for an early break in the case." Looking at the pavement, with his hands in his pockets searching for his ever-present antacids, he was too preoccupied to see the flock of village children who scurried along beside them.

"I'm beginning to agree with that Ms. Smith that everyone in this village is looney," said the inspector.

Unlike his superior, Officer Rogers found it difficult to ignore the youngsters. Knowing full well the reason for the presence of the Scotland Yard men they barraged him with questions while the very young ones tugged at his coat. He playfully bantered with them encouraging their liveliness.

The inspector finally noticed their presence and with a menacing voice, ordered them to disperse.

Officer Rogers, laughed and said, "Maybe you'll feel better after lunch sir. Wc can grab a bite at the pub." Aware of his superior's apathetic attitude towards food he quickly added, "We can discuss our interviews while we eat."

"I've already got a blinking headache, I don't need an upset stomach to go with it," replied the inspector brusquely. "We can discuss the case *after* we eat."

The two policemen made their way across the village green in the direction of the pub with a few of the older and braver youngsters following at a distance.

Inside the busy pub, the children's antics were replaced with stares and an awkward silence from the pub patrons as the policemen wound their way to a secluded table in the corner. The landlord, a jovial, good natured native of the village, hastened to their table with two half pints in hand in an attempt to deflect the awkwardness.

Gratefully accepting the beer, both police officers ordered sausage pasties - the house specialty.

As it was the lunch hour, the pub was quickly filling up with regulars. With their lunch in front of them, the two policemen gratefully dug in. Inspector Bunson mechanically ate his afternoon meal, and made a concentrated effort to keep his eyes on his plate not wishing to engage in any village gossip.

Conscious of the Inspector's silence, Sergeant Rogers knew that this meant the Inspector was more than a little concerned about the direction the case was taking. He also knew better than to try to elicit conversation when the Inspector was in this mood. His Sergeant's salary barely allowed him to pay his rent, living expenses in London and his one extravagance, a two-year old Boxer named Jasper whom he spoiled as if a child. So the expense account lunches were much appreciated. He was grateful for the generous portions served at the pub and he sat quietly eating while mulling over the recent interviews.

Looking up at one point, Officer Rogers saw Sam Taylor entering the pub. Sam, a normally friendly and outgoing person, curtly nodded in greeting as he caught Rogers' eye and then promptly headed towards the opposite end of the bar.

"How about another sausage pie to take home to your monster?" offered Inspector Bunson noting that Rogers had practically licked his plate clean.

"No, but thanks just the same, Inspector, you know Jasper only eats prime sirloin. Pork doesn't agree with him – gives him indigestion," replied Rogers.

"I also know that that brute eats, guinea hen, salmon, any and all chops and I wouldn't be surprised if you buy fois gras for him," rallied the Inspector.

Unabashed the Sergeant replied, "Oh, no you're wrong about the fois gras, Inspector. Jasper hasn't experienced that delicacy yet."

As they walked to the exit, they passed Sam who was seated at a table speaking with Jim McCarthy, the editor of the village paper.

Noticing the police officers, Jim quickly got up and asked if they'd be willing to meet with him later that day at the police station.

By late afternoon, Inspector Bunson and Officer Rogers were going through the preliminary reports and interviews in their makeshift office in the tiny village police station. They hadn't gotten far when a constable announced that Jim McCarthy was waiting to see them.

Upon being shown into the office, Jim McCarthy immediately got to the point of his visit. "Thanks for seeing me, Inspector. I actually have a favor to ask of you and I won't beat about the bush. I came here to ask if it wouldn't be against procedural policy for you to allow me to print on-going details of the case. I don't mean for you to take me into your confidence, I understand that's not an option considering the circumstances." He looked self-consciously at Officer Rogers who was pursing his lips and looking at the inspector.

"I'd like to help you, Mr. McCarthy, I understand your paper's been a great asset to the town in many ways. And you've an excellent reputation in the field," replied Bunson, "I also understand that the public must have its news – especially when it's so near to home." Then putting his fingertips together he sat in silent contemplation.

After a couple of minutes, the Inspector rose, walked around to the front of his desk and said, "I think it would be in the best interests of all parties if we agreed to collaborate. We will be happy to give your readers updates on our progress in the case."

The editor almost jumped from his seat in his excitement and shaking the inspector's hand, said "Thanks so much Inspector, I have a feeling that a column or two might even reach London! I don't mean to be morbid but, *'Suspicious Death of Vicar's Spinster Sister In Rural Countryside Village'* will make great copy. And who knows, it might even lead to a break in the case," he added enthusiastically.

"It will be a collaboration Mr. McCarthy. We expect you to give all pertinent information you might happen to come across," replied Inspector Bunson.

Chapter 11

The funeral of Julia Peters took place the following day. To the dismay of Cornelia and Jack, who enjoyed trekking around the village, the countryside awoke to a steady downpour that came down in horizontal fashion thanks to a gale force wind.

Susana, who was not one to do any exercise if she could help it, greeted her siblings as they came down for breakfast. "Ooh, can you hear that howling wind? I'm so glad we won't have to walk through the village this morning. I really was not looking forward to ruining another pair of shoes on our country roads. It's kind of scary – don't funerals in horror movies always have weather like this?"

"If you'd buy yourself a pair of sensible brogues you wouldn't have those worries," said Cornelia looking down with dismay at Susana's dainty pumps.

"And you wouldn't have to keep sending your shoes out for repairs," added Jack with a smile.

Susana's good humor was not easily squelched and she replied, "Yes, I know you're both right but walking shoes are so heavy they make my feet hurt. And don't tell me to get sneakers! The don't match any of my outfits – or do they?"

As they approached the kitchen, Jack suddenly stopped and said, "Hey, is that real coffee I smell? I mean coffee that's not burned?"

"Oh dear, something must be wrong with Martha," expressed a worried Susana entering the kitchen.

"Mmmm, that coffee smells delicious. I wonder who made it?" voiced Jack out loud while going to the coffeemaker and pouring three mugs.

From the pantry emerged a young, girl in her late teens.

"Hello Pinkey, nice to see you! Did you make the coffee?" evoked Jack sitting down at the kitchen table.

Having lived in the village of Epping all of her life Pinkey Clark was a familiar face. Pinkey was Martha's sister's daughter and as shy and quiet as Martha was loud and extroverted. "Aunty Martha told me to tell you that she's gonna be sleeping at our house on account of being too frightened of the mad killer coming here at night and strangling her," replied Pinkey twisting her pony tail into a knot. "She said to tell you that she'll be coming up at noon and leaving again before it gets dark." Pinkey, who was the only Jenkins with normal intelligence, rolled her eyes up to heaven.

"Yep, sounds like Martha," laughed Jack. "Well there goes our peace and quiet," observed Cornelia in hushed tones.

Pinkey, purposely avoiding eye contact with the siblings continued, "Aunty Martha said to tell you that since she'll be leaving right after tea not to expect her to do any cooking." Thankfully not having inherited her aunt's limited intelligence, Pinkey added shyly, "I won't be starting my job at the grocer's 'til next month so I'd be more than willing to help here."

Susana went up to the girl and with a kind smile said, "Well of course dear, we would be very grateful for your help. You can help me in the kitchen and be my sous chef."

"You mean be your assistant?" asked a delighted Pinkey.

"Most definitely! If you'd like, you can begin your duties immediately. Is that alright?" replied Susana and she grabbed her apron and headed for the pantry.

By ten o'clock with Jack behind the wheel of the Rover the three siblings were on their way to the funeral. The rain had now turned into a downpour with intermittent gales turning the narrow country lanes into winding brooks littered with tree branches.

Looking out the window, Susana pulled her coat tighter around her and made sure the scarf she wore around her neck was firmly secured by her mother's pearl pin. She was baffled by Cornelia's pensive mood and said, "I know we're paying our last respects to Julia but no matter how hard I try I really can't feel very sorry that she's gone. I didn't know you felt her passing so deeply Cornelia. Am I rotten to not grieve?"

Her sister made a sound closely resembling a guffaw, "Oh, no, it's not that. I've just been wondering how far Inspector Bunson is getting in his investigations. Not very pleasant to think that we're burying Julia because someone whom we know has done away with her."

"I didn't want to verbalize it but now that you mentioned it, we have to admit that we have a murderer in our midst," replied Jack swerving around a large tree branch.

"My goodness Jack can't you be more careful?" exclaimed Susana.

"Sorry, didn't see that branch from the bend in the road," replied Jack.

"I didn't mean that, I was referring to the word '*murder*' – it's so graphic. And anyway, I refuse to believe that someone whom we might call a friend – and was in our home - had anything to do with Julia's death," answered Susana.

"Susana's right," observed a contemplative Cornelia. "How can we be living with a mur...I mean, poisoner whom we might meet up with at anytime?"

"We don't have a choice considering we have no idea who the poisoner is," said Jack sarcastically.

"Yes, that does make things difficult," observed Cornelia thoughtfully.

If Julia's popularity while alive was to be measured by the attendance at her funeral, then one would have to say that she was not an endeared member of the community. Aside from her brother, the only other mourners included the Leslie siblings, Phyllis Stavis, Debra O'Neil, Sam Taylor, and Jim McCarthy. The latter having attended in the hope of obtaining material for his newspaper. The others were present out of respect for Reverend Peters.

The lashing rain had thankfully stopped and dark clouds formed an eerie backdrop around the small gathering paying their last respects with the autumn leaves swirling around their feet. The women instinctively huddled around the vicar and at the end of the services, performed by a neighboring priest, the party rapidly walked to the vicarage, under the surveillance of a large crowd of curious villagers who had gathered behind the low walls of the cemetery.

Inspector Bunson and Officer Rogers were also present at the cemetery however their presence was in an official capacity and although they witnessed the service from inside the cemetery walls, they remained at a polite distance. Observing the mourners as they wound their way to the vicarage, Inspector Bunson turned to his Sergeant and asked what time lunch was served at the elementary school.

"Didn't you like the fare served at the Raven's Roost?" joked Sergeant Rogers. When he didn't get a reply from his superior he decided to try a more businesslike approach, "I believe the school serves lunch at one o'clock. Are we going to go interview the teachers, sir?"

"*One* teacher, Sergeant. But I'd like to have my lunch before we go. We have just enough time to swallow a few bites," replied a somber Inspector with his nose twitching.

The village elementary school had been built in the late 19th century as the village's main schoolhouse containing both the elementary and high school within its four rooms. Since then it had suffered at least four renovations. The growth of the village and town necessitated the building of a middle school and high school and the original schoolhouse was now used solely as the elementary school.

"I don't know how you can eat so much in so little time," said Inspector Bunson to Officer Rogers as they came out of the Raven's Roost. "Don't you have even the slightest indigestion?" The Inspector was looking a little uncomfortable himself. He was one of those odd characters who eat to live and have very little interest in food itself. He learned early in his association with the younger detective to keep a supply of antacids with him at all times.

"Heck, I grew up eating on the run. My mum worked all day and we rushed through breakfast so she could drive me to school and get to work. Then after school I went to daycare until she picked me up to go to the town diner to eat. Now I get up, rush to get my java with a bagel or egg sandwich, and in the evening, I stop at the market to buy dinner for me and Jasper, or if I've had a long day, I stop for fast food and defrost a steak for Jasper and we eat while he watches the telly and I work on the computer."

Wincing in pain, Inspector Bunson looked at his Sergeant and said, "Please, Sergeant let's not go into too much detail."

The secretary at the elementary school who was herself an institution at the school having held that position for more years than anyone cared to remember looked up from her desk to find Officer Rogers standing in front of her.

The tiny white haired old lady gave him a beaming smile, "Hello Michael, I've been reading all about you in the papers. It sounds so exciting...and a little spooky!" she gushed at Officer Rogers.

Sergeant Rogers, noting the amusement on his superior's face, turned a deep red and said, "Yes, well that's why Inspector Bunson and I are here Miss Briggs. Is there any way we can speak with Betty Smith?

"Of course! We were so lucky she was still in town. Phyllis Stavis hired her you know when our third grade teacher, Mrs. Olive had to have an emergency appendectomy," she replied going up to the Inspector to shake hands. "I'm such a fan of suspense novels – nothing like reading about murder while sitting in a cozy chair by the fire – it's my favorite hobby and now there's a mysterious death right in our village. If you need any help, anything at all, please just ask. I'd be thrilled to assist!" Miss Briggs managed to get all this out in almost one breath while vigorously shaking the Inspector's hand.

It was Officer Rogers' turn to smile while the Inspector tried to find a suitable reply.

The detectives were taken to a conference room by Miss Briggs who made it a point to inform their identities to every adult along the way. They didn't have to wait very long before Betty entered holding a cafeteria tray.

"I hope you don't mind but I was in the middle of my lunch. They don't give us more than a half hour," she said apologetically.

"You have our apologies for barging in on you during your lunch break Ms. Smith. I hope that this won't take too much time. We're just following up on the preliminary reports," offered the Inspector while Officer Rogers pulled out a chair at the table for the teacher.

Betty Smith smiled pleasantly, "Don't apologize, I really shouldn't be eating all this food. It's not that appetizing when it's being served and even less so once it's on the tray!" she gave a nervous laugh.

"I know exactly what you mean," chuckled the Inspector gazing at the plates on the tray and trying to guess what they contained. He recognized the neon green wobbling square and hoped it was only '*Jello*' then immediately felt a stabbing pain in his stomach.

Betty sat moving a red and white mass of food in artistic circles around a plate avoiding eye contact with either of the policemen. She looked both unhappy and preoccupied. It took a loud throat clearing from the inspector before she heard the question about owning a car.

Giving herself a slight shake, she answered, "Yes, of course. I own a small Honda Fit. It's my main link to civilization."

Inspector Bunson furrowed his brow for a few seconds before he was able to figure out her meaning. "By that I suppose you mean that you use it primarily for pleasure?" he asked uncertainly.

Once again, Betty was not listening. She had moved on to another plate that contained a brown lump oozing a gooey pink liquid that she was trying unsuccessfully to mash together. The Inspector made a good-natured face at the plate and commented that the pink ooze was most likely related to plastic.

This produced the desired effect and Betty looked up with a laugh.

"Could you explain what you meant when you said that your car is your link to civilization?" asked a patient Inspector Bunson.

"Nothing really. But if you must know, there's precious little nightlife around here. The closest nightclub is in London for heaven's sake."

A loud piercing bell sounded and Betty immediately got up saying, "Well, that's the end of my break. Sorry but I've got to get back to my students." With that she walked to the door and into the onslaught in the hall while the Inspector and Sergeant remained hidden behind the door. With the sound of a second bell, the hall was deserted and the detectives were able to come out of hiding.

"She's keeping something from us, Inspector," observed Officer Rogers as soon as he had dislodged himself from Miss Briggs and was safely outside.

"Oh, really? Tell me, how did you come to that electrifying conclusion?" asked the Inspector sarcastically.

"Then if you don't mind me asking, sir, why didn't we keep questioning her until we found out why she's so nervous?" asked a bewildered Sergeant.

"Because, if you weren't listening, she had 'to get back to her students'. Well, we can worry about that later. Now I'd like to go have a talk with the Reverend Peters," replied the inspector thoughtfully.

The sergeant couldn't help but notice the twitching of his superior's nose.

Chapter 12

On the afternoon of Julia Peters' funeral, Cornelia and Jack sat in the library enjoying a cocktail. Susana, who had stayed up late the night before researching her vast cookbook collection for recipes that she would use for the week, was busy in the kitchen cooking and overseeing Pinkey's introduction to French cuisine.

"I eat potatoes all the time and I know that leeks are those green onions on steroids but I've never heard of a soup called 'Bitchy Wives'," said Pinkey as she chopped potatoes and leeks.

If there was anything Susana enjoyed more than cooking it was teaching the art of cooking. Hearing Pinkey's creative name for 'Vichyssoise', she chuckled and explained the correct name before saying she preferred Pinkey's version of the soup's name much better.

In the library, Cornelia steeled herself to ask her brother about Betty. "Did you get into a fight with Betty?" she asked him over the rim of her martini.

"No, why do you ask?" replied Jack avoiding eye contact by walking over to a bookshelf and taking a protracted look at a large tome.

"Well, she was here for the weekend and then all of a sudden she's gone, that's all. I don't mean to be a nosey parker," said Cornelia enjoying her martini.

Jack put the book down and came over to a chair near Cornelia. "It was just simpler to have her here that weekend. You and Susana were away and I was planning the dinner party and I thought Betty might like to help in the preparations."

"And did she help?" she asked skeptically.

"No, not really. She's not the homebody type. And actually I should have known better because on more than one occasion she's asked me to go up to London with her for the weekend." Cornelia raised her eyebrows ever so slightly. Jack continued, "She runs with a pretty fast crowd up there."

Cornelia smiled and nodded. "She must miss London quite a lot if she's as outgoing as you say." Then as if to herself she asked, "I wonder why she came down to this part of the world?" and went out to see what Susana was concocting in the kitchen.

She found Pinkey, studiously dredging Dover sole filets in flour and seasonings while Susana stood by the stove sauteing the filets in butter.

"My favorite fish!" exclaimed Cornelia approvingly then addressing Pinkey she asked, "Are you enjoying being a sous chef, Pinkey?"

"Oh yes, Mrs. C.! I'm learning so much, and this is only my first lesson! Just standing here watching Mrs. S. sowtay the 'Soul Manure' is making my mouth water! I didn't know fish could smell so good!" replied Pinkey enthusiastically.

"Pinkey's been a marvelous assistant, Cornelia. She's enthusiastic and she's a quick learner – would you believe her *'Sole Meunier'* has turned out better than mine?"

Pinkey, turning beet red, smiled happily.

The vicarage was located at the other end of the village from the elementary school. When Sergeant Rogers headed for the police car, he was informed by the Inspector that since it wasn't raining, a nice walk through the village seemed an ideal way for the inspector to get the flavor of village life. As they walked past houses the fluttering of curtains and the sudden rush to do a bit of gardening by curious residents made their progress entertaining. Several times, the ever-popular Sergeant was greeted from behind hedges or around rose bushes with eager faces seeking a bit of news. Crossing an old stone bridge the Inspector stopped to look down at the water. Although it was called a river, the water gurgled slowly under them in a shallow green pool.

"The kids swim a little further down where it gets deeper," volunteered the sergeant, "It's lovely here in the Spring and Summer, the water is cold but clear enough that you can see down into the sand clear as day."

Just past the bridge, the Inspector spotted the Norman tower of St. Mary's Church and next door the Victorian era vicarage. The small church had won acclaim with its pure thirteenth century Norman style both inside and out. During the tourist season, the church grounds were continuously trampled by masses of tourists. The vicarage on the other hand, was a large grey mass with ugly asymmetric bulging windows and misplaced balconies. There were missing slate tiles on the roof and it was obvious that maintenance was not a high priority.

The inspector shuddered as he approached the ugly building and said, "I don't even want to think how much it costs to heat that place. It's got to be full of drafts."

As they got closer, a figure in the side garden could be seen hanging the wash on an old-fashioned clothesline.

Unlike the house, the garden was immaculately maintained and the scent of late blooming roses gave a heady perfume.

"That'll be Mrs. Hardy from the next town over." explained Officer Rogers. "She's the latest in a long line of housekeepers."

The two policemen walked up the stone path towards the front door. Inspector Bunson stopped suddenly. "I'm used to bystanders staring but we didn't let anyone know about our coming this way. Was there any advance warning?" he asked his Sergeant.

"That's known as the *'village telegraph'*. Around here news travels fast." chuckled Rogers in reply.

At the end of the path they came up to four steps leading up to a dark porch that contained a single wicker chair. The sergeant pressed his finger on the bell and immediately the sound of Wagner's *'Ride of the Valkyries'* could be heard inside.

"What in heaven's name is that?" asked the inspector who had been taken unawares.

Officer Rogers who had been eagerly anticipating this moment gave a wry laugh and said, "That was Julia's pride and joy. She had it installed the day she moved in. Takes you off guard doesn't it?"

From inside a loud voice could be heard approaching the door while giving its opinion about what it thought of Wagner's opus. The door was opened by a large, middle-aged woman wearing a pristine white apron.

"Sorry about the noise. I don't know why the Reverend Peters doesn't take that blastin' clamor down now. It's enough to split your head wide open with the crashin' and clangin'." Then she stopped and straightening her apron said, "You must be the Scotland Yard Inspector…and Mikey! Well, come on in, I know what you've come about."

The inspector wondered out loud how she had managed to get from hanging clothes outside to answering the front door so fast not to mention knowing who they were.

Trying to keep a straight face, Officer Rogers nudged his superior officer and mouthed, '*village telegraph*'.

Ignoring his sergeant and attempting to look dignified, the Inspector replied, "Ahem, yes, that's right, if you would kindly let Reverend Peters know we're here."

"Oh that's too bad, he's not here," Mrs. Hardy's bright eyes and cheerful expression nullified her words of regret, "Went to town to the nursery there. Likes to spend all morning talkin' about vegetables and flowers with the owner. Of course now that Miss Peters isn't around he has a chance to do that," she snorted.

The off-hand remark did not go unnoticed by Inspector Bunson and he told himself that he would need to speak to his sergeant about setting up a time to meet with Mrs. Hardy. This thought barely passed before Mrs. Hardy eagerly expressed her wish to have them come in to the kitchen for tea.

The detectives entered a dimly lit entry hall that bore the green paint typical of early twentieth century institutions. The room had little trace of any personal effects and any light coming in through two tiny windows was obstructed by heavy, brown curtains. Closing the door she turned towards an even darker, narrow passage and motioned them to follow. The inspector noticed that despite the housekeeper's heavy build she had a remarkably quick gait.

"You're just in time for some nice scones fresh out of the oven," she said chattily.

The inspector's earlier remark about heat and draughts became sorely apparent. The corridor was like a wind tunnel that seemed colder than the temperature outside. Mrs. Hardy suddenly disappeared out of view at a bend in the corridor. When the police officers caught up they were in an unexpectedly bright and cheery kitchen with the delicious aroma of freshly baked goods.

"Warm your bodies there by the fire," motioned Mrs. Hardy, "I know how glacial it is outside of this room."

"You mean the rest of the house is as cold as that passage?" asked the inspector in disbelief as he stood in front of the blazing fire trying to get warm.

Hungrily focusing on the fragrant scones Mrs. Hardy was setting on a large oak table that looked as if it had once belonged in a monastery Rogers said, "I forgot how cold this place is. When we were kids we thought that it was because it was haunted. Of course that was years ago" he said self-consciously.

Mrs. Hardy laughed and lowering her voice to a conspiratorial whisper said, "I know we mustn't speak ill of the dead, but between you and me, it's some of the live ones that do the hauntin' – if you get my meanin'."

Gratefully cognizant that he was given a clear opportunity to continue the conversation along the same lines, Inspector Bunter nodded his head in agreement,

"Some people are born angry," he said as he moved to the table.

"Isn't that the truth! Take my Henry, husband you know, he was born a saint. So long as he can watch or read about his football teams he's happy. His brother on the other hand was only happy when he was miserable and makin' other people miserable," she added shaking her head as she handed the officers steaming mugs of black tea and pushed the platter of scones towards them. "Might as well enjoy them while they're hot, no one else is goin' to eat them in this house."

Mounding butter on his third scone, Sergeant Rogers looked wide-eyed, "These are the best scones I've tasted in a long time Mrs. Hardy, I can't believe the vicar would pass them up."

"You'd be surprised," began Mrs. Hardy as she settled herself for a cozy chat, "That man lives on cups of sweet, black tea. Of course when she was alive, she'd sit at the big desk in the library every Monday mornin' giving me the week's menu. I could hardly believe it, the food wasn't enough to feed a child of two! Then instead of allowin' me to do the shoppin' as in most households I've worked in, she'd have me give her a list of ingredients and she'd end up bringing the cheapest cut of beef, chicken or fish. The vegetables were shriveled and don't even ask me about the fruit because she never bought any! I'd start havin' anxiety attacks every Sunday evenin' just thinkin' about Monday, I can tell you!"

Inspector Bunson was also enjoying the scones piled high with homemade raspberry preserves. Observing that Mrs. Hardy was happily giving details of her employers without having to be prodded, he had remained silent making appreciative noises at various intervals.

A stunned Rogers asked, "You mean she was starving the vicar?"

Gratified at the interest that she had elicited, Mrs. Hardy shook her wobbly chins for added emphasis. "As I said before, she was one of those who get pleasure makin' others miserable. I can't tell you how many times I'd buy a little somethin' extra for the man, all skin and bones that he is, as a treat you know, and she'd make such a scene that he'd just lose all appetite. Makes one wonder doesn't it?"

The inspector felt as though he were swimming in tea. He had drunk at least two large mugs and eaten four scones. When he was pressed by Mrs. Hardy with a third mug of tea he haltingly accepted not willing to stem the flow of information from the housekeeper.

"I have the impression that Miss Peters was somewhat controlling," he prompted.

"That's an understatement if I ever heard one." she said flatly. "The way she ordered the poor man around! It wasn't enough that her brother was the vicar and a leading member of the community. Why the poor soul couldn't wear an old, comfy sweater in his own home on account of she'd hiss at him to change into somethin' *'more dignified'*." Again the chins quivered. "This house is called the vicarage, but the poor vicar was never in charge of anythin'. Do you know who had use of the study?" Not waiting for a reply she said, "It wasn't the vicar, he'd have to sit in a small desk in that freezin' front room which is colder than the north o' Scotland to write his sermons while she held court at the big desk in the study giving orders to her underlings at the

Women's Institute and all those other committees she headed." Mrs. Hardy stopped to take a breath but decided against it and continued her monologue, "From dawn to dusk that woman would follow her brother around chastisin' him for any little thing." After finally stopping to take a breath she went on, "Do you know what I think?"

For once it was the inspector who was caught with a mouthful of food so Officer Rogers attempted to answer, "Wha..."

Mrs. Hardy didn't wait to hear, "That man is a saint to have lived with that gargoyle all this time." Tea from Mrs. Hardy's mug splattered on the table as she banged the mug down to emphasize her point.

Inspector Bunson maintained an expression of astonishment coupled with disbelief for the benefit of Mrs. Hardy. He now rose, albeit with a little difficulty with the tea sloshing in his stomach, and thanking the housekeeper for a very excellent tea he and Sergeant Rogers left the vicarage.

Chapter 13

Having attended Julia's funeral and then walked back to the vicarage with the other mourners, Jim McCarthy and Sam Taylor crossed the village to the Raven's Roost. The pub at that hour was deserted and Bert Colby, who at that moment was wondering how he was going to pay for his daughter's dental work greeted them with a hearty welcome.

"I don't blame you fellows comin' in here for a pint. Funerals have a way of makin' one thirsty and I'm sure our Miss Julia's was no different," he said in his typecast bonhomie manner.

Sam and Jim both nodded assent, grateful to be out of the funereal atmosphere. "The vicar's taking Julia's passing much harder than I expected. Let's hope he doesn't land in hospital," said Sam reaching for his glass.

"Yeah, it's difficult to see him this way," agreed Jim. "But you'd think that after all the funeral services that he's presided over and all the support he's given to grieving families, he'd be able to handle it better. I feel for him."

The amiable landlord of the Raven's Roost, listened intently considering it part and parcel of running a successful pub. Conversely, his patrons knew that anything said in the bar was held in the same context as the confessional and they were glad to mix pints with sensible, country wisdom freely handed out by the landlord. It was well known that Bert Colby knew more about the lives of his neighbors than anyone else.

"Our Julia wasn't exactly *Mother Teresa.* But I guess family is family and you know what they say, blood is thicker than water," he said trying to sound philosophical.

Jim laughed, "That's just it, I always had the impression that Julia bullied her brother. I found him to be on pins and needles around her and it made me uncomfortable being with the vicar when his sister was present."

"She certainly was difficult to deal with," said Sam with a resigned sigh as he finished his beer.

"Seems a shame you won't be getting that piece of land over by the church Sam. But I guess the town needs to expand the cemetery," said the editor conversationally.

Sam waited a couple of minutes before answering and then said, "I was always under the impression that there was still plenty of open space in the present cemetery," and walked out of the pub without finishing his beer.

Jim stood at the bar, picked up his glass and after downing the beer said to no one in particular, "I believe it's time to have a conversation with a few people."

"Thank you Susana, I really enjoyed that," said Jack as he swallowed the last mouthful of tender sole. "It's a miracle we're all still alive having eaten Martha's cooking for so long," he added with a grin.

"I'm very hopeful that Pinkey will turn out to

be a very competent cook and then it shouldn't be difficult to enlist her to 'assist' Martha with her duties in the kitchen," commented Susana. "In fact she almost made the dessert all by herself tonight. Isn't that wonderful?"

"I'm sure that whatever the dessert is it will be delicious but I really must catch up on my work which I've let slide with all that's happened in the last few days. All I can say is that I'm lucky I can work from home." He bent down to kiss his sisters and walked to the dining room door, turned and said, "Oh by the way, Debra O'Neil called this afternoon wondering if you two would like to have lunch with her and Phyllis tomorrow. She said she'd call again in the morning." And with that he left the dining room and headed for the library.

"Let's go to the kitchen and get dessert, although I ate so much fish I doubt if I have room!" said Cornelia,

"Alright, we can take it upstairs along with our Ovaltine. I've been waiting all evening to tell you something that Pinkey told me. I didn't want to bring it up in front of Jack. He's so suspicious isn't he?" said Susana mysteriously.

Carrying trays with desserts and Ovaltine, the sisters bid their brother good night with reminders from each of them to make sure that he walk around the house checking that all windows and doors be securely locked up for the night. After getting reassurances that he wouldn't go to bed until he was satisfied that the house was sealed like Fort Knox, they made their way upstairs.

As was their custom since childhood, Cornelia first went to her room, got into her pajamas and then walked across the hall to her sister's room. She settled herself in the overstuffed pink and cream divan covering herself with a pink cashmere throw while Susana readied herself for bed.

"Darn, I knew I should have served myself a bigger slice!" exclaimed Cornelia wiping whipped cream from the side of her mouth, "I never serve myself enough when we bring dessert upstairs."

"Well you can always run down and help yourself to seconds, Cornelia, can't you?" replied Susana with a smile of satisfaction as she looked down on her own double helping.

"But I'm so comfortable now and besides, since you always have more than enough for two people, I'll just have some of yours," she added cagily.

"Cornelia that's not fair. Just because you didn't have foresight that you'd want more doesn't mean that I'll give you some of mine," answered Susana with feeling. "You can go on down to the kitchen and serve yourself as much as you want. The hall light's still on isn't it?"

"Oh alright. But first tell me what Pinkey said."

"Ohh, I almost forgot! And it was on my mind all through dinner. Really, I'm so impressed with that girl. It's a wonder that she's at all related to Martha. Strange isn't it?" answered Susana chattily.

"You can't be serious, that's what you've been waiting to tell me all evening?" asked and incredulous Cornelia.

"Of course not, silly. Have you ever noticed your habit of mixing up thoughts?" replied Susana giving her sister a worried look.

"Oh for heavens sake, Susana, try not to ramble and tell me what Pinkey said. The Ovaltine has made me drowsy and I'm having trouble keeping my eyes opened," replied an exasperated Cornelia.

"Alright, alright calm down I'm getting there," replied Susana taking a dainty bite of dessert. Then adjusting her pink satin bed jacket and leaning back on the pillows she continued, "Well, as we all know, Pinkey was spared from inheriting the Jenkins' mental deficiency - thankfully for her. But she does like to gab about anything and everything, just like all the Jenkins. Well, as we were cooking dinner, she told me that her mother and Martha are always fighting. Actually Pinkey called it 'cat fighting'." Susana screwed up her face in thought, "Remember how when they were growing up they'd always be shouting and screaming at each other Cornelia? Now that I think of it, they did sound like cats. Well anyway, Pinkey said that the night before last, Martha threw a pot at Pinkey's mother and missed her head by inches and the night before that she had hysterics about being the next to be killed by the 'psycho-maniac killer'!" exclaimed Susana. Then with an involuntary shiver asked, "Actually, Cornelia, I don't blame her do you?"

Cornelia's mouth quivered as she tried to present a serious face in response to her sister's story. "You know as well as I do how easily bizarre ideas take root in Martha's idle brain. That family's as screwy as they come. They always were and always will be," and with that, Cornelia slowly stood up. "I'm going to bed Susana, it's been a long day and the emotions of the past couple of days are wearing on me."

Susana sat up and protested, "Oh but Cornelia, I'm not finished with my story!"

Rubbing her eyes and yawning Cornelia

dropped into the divan and replied, "Okay, but hurry it up."

"Get this," replied Susana assuming a dramatically serious expression and squinting her eyes, "Pinkey's mom told her that Martha's all in a dither because she's afraid of something. And that something is a *someone*. And that someone has a name. And that name is known to Martha!" Susana gave a dramatic shudder, "Isn't that scary?"

Cornelia was now wide awake. "Someone should tell that family that they talk too much for their own good and it's going to get them into trouble one of these days," and with that she walked out of the room.

Chapter 14

The following morning, after speaking on the phone with the Chief Constable, Inspector Bunson sat at his desk staring out the window. His focus was not on the wind that was wreaking havoc on the trees but on the story printed in the latest edition of the 'Town Crier'.

Jim McCarthy had ill-advisedly printed a story citing the donation of land as the primary motive in the death of Julia Peters. Major Sandowne, the Chief Constable, had asked the Inspector why he wasn't given the stunning piece of information before it was sent to the paper.

After considerable mental aerobics, Inspector Bunson was able to dissuade the Chief Constable of the notion that he was responsible for the paper's thrilling yet misguided story. To his credit, Major Sandown voiced the opinion that newspapermen were capable of selling their own mothers for a sensational front page story. At the end of the phone call the Inspector was left with a drenched shirt and thoughts of revoking his promise to Jim McCarthy with respect to advance police information.

"Sorry I'm a bit late, Inspector," said Rogers, dropping his car keys, and a brown paper bag onto the desk across from the inspector.

"What in the world do you have in your hand and don't tell me you intend to drink all that in one day?" asked a wide-eyed inspector looking at a large container which the Sergeant was holding.

"It's called a 'venti', Inspector. I believe that's Italian for twenty which probably refers to the number of ounces of java it contains," replied Rogers eager to illuminate the Inspector on proper cafe lingo. "It's the reason I'm late."

"Long lines of coffee aficionados?" asked Inspector Bunson facetiously.

"Not more than usual," began the Sergeant immune to subtle quips which his good natured temperament made difficult to penetrate, "No, my fault entirely. You see I got up extra early to make Jasper a special breakfast on account of it being his half birthday today."

The inspector looked at his Sergeant with a faint grin developing on his face. Here he was, just having been more or less told by his Chief Constable that the case he was heading was being mismanaged and he was actually enjoying an idiotic story about a dog's half-birthday breakfast!

Once started on the topic of his dog, Sergeant Rogers was difficult to stop. "I had a thick, juicy rib eye steak grilled to perfection – kind of underdone just like Jasper likes it–which I was plating. Well I guess Jasper was just too hungry to wait for me to set it down and he grabbed the steak, plate and all, out of my hands. You should have seen how quickly he ate that steak and boy did he enjoy it!" beamed the Sergeant. Inspector Bunson reflected that a father broadcasting the first steps of his child could not
have looked any prouder. Sergeant Rogers opened

the brown bag that contained a fried egg sandwich and pushing aside folders sat down on his desk and began eating. "So, what's on for today, Inspector?" he asked taking a huge swallow of coffee.

The inspector was jolted back to earth from his reverie of huge dogs and mountains of food. "I was thinking that you might call Jim McCarthy and ask him to come down to the station," he replied.

"I guess you saw this morning's paper. It's amazing the lengths that journalists will go to sell a paper. But I can't blame him too much, I mean the guy's a good newspaperman and he's taking advantage of the biggest story ever to come out of this town," replied the Sergeant in between bites.

Still wincing from that morning's conversation with the Chief Constable, Inspector Bunson turned his indignation on his Sergeant, "If it's not too much to ask, when you're finished stuffing your face you can call him and tell him that if he isn't here in the next thirty minutes, he won't have any more stories to print."

"Cornelia, I wish you wouldn't always be so health conscious. It can't possibly be good for you, you know. I mean all this walking when it's just as easy or easier really, to drive. Aren't your feet killing you?" huffed Susana as she tried to keep up with her sister's brisk pace.

They had made arrangements to meet Debra and Phyllis at the Tarts and Buns for lunch and Cornelia had suggested walking to the teashop.

"There's nothing healthier than walking especially for people our age, Susana, so stop complaining. Besides, if we walk to our lunch think of how much we'll be able to eat!" replied Cornelia bending down to inspect a rose as she waited for Susana to catch up.

"You've got a point there. I do look forward to Nora's cooking. She was so clever to add a lunch menu to her already delicious baked goods. After all, she does deserve to be happy and it's not every woman who has the courage to start a business of her own. Don't you think?"

"Nora had no choice. She was forced to quit her job in that fancy London bakery because they refused to pay her a fair salary even though it was her baking that was bringing in all the customers. I hope they're regretting their actions," replied her sister.

"Oh I know! I heard that the owner of the bakery actually tried to hang around the 'Tarts and Buns' asking to speak to Nora saying that he was sorry and wanted to make up with her until she called Constable Jenkins who practically had to carry him off the premises. Isn't that just too much?"

"Ha! Serves him right. Their profits probably took a dive while from the looks of things here, Nora's doing a stellar business," replied her sister as they turned the corner and came onto Main Street.

Susana had not heard her sister's last remark as her attention was focused on the window of the village store.

"Cornelia look! This is terrible! I was too busy explaining tonight's dinner to Pinkey that I didn't have a chance to look at the morning paper. It's too devastating for words that our gift of land to the town should be the reason behind Julia's death. Can you believe it?" exclaimed a distraught Susana.

Cornelia was captivated by the article but fter a few jabs from her sister, she responded, "It certainly is intriguing. I would think that this means the police have narrowed down their suspects."

Inside the teashop, Cornelia made her way to the table where Debra and Phyllis were already seated while Susana took a detour to the pastry display case.

"Hullo Ginny," she greeted one of the two shop assistants, "Ohhh the creamed horns look scrumptious, look at all that cream! I suppose one of them would be enough to completely block my arteries," she said with sigh. Then taking in the rest of the display, wondered out loud, "Why can't pastries be healthy?"

Lunch at the Tarts and Buns was in the continental style with a pris fix menu consisting of a choice between two entrees, a salad and any dessert from the case. The women concentrated their gaze on the blackboard printed with the day's specials.

"Nora has *'Shepherd's Pie'* on the board – I'm all set," said Phyllis as Ginny approached their table to take their order.

"That does sound yummy but I'll go with the *'Quiche Lorraine'* and salad," said Debra.

"I'd love to just order desserts for my lunch," quipped Susana. "But I guess I'll have the quiche and salad so that I won't feel too guilty when I do order dessert. Aren't I awful?" she laughed.

"Make that three quiches Ginny," said Cornelia.

"And how about a bottle of the house *Pinot Grigot?*" asked Phyllis looking at the rest of the women then quickly added, "You can close your mouth now Ginny, I was just kidding. We're all having lemonade."

When Ginny had left to take their orders to the kitchen, Debra said, "According to the article in the paper, we could all be possible suspects. I really can't imagine anyone in the village killing Julia over a piece of land."

"The formal forensic finding is that she was poisoned. That means that someone had to have administered the poison – unless she took her own life which knowing Julia, is highly unlikely," replied Cornelia.

"Exactly. Translation: She was murdered – and let's not be hypocrites – almost everyone in the village had a pretty good reason to detest Julia," pronounced Phyllis emphatically.

"To put it bluntly, I'd say that Julia was hated if not despised by the villagers. Even with all her chairmanships she was divisive and enjoyed using her position as sister to the Vicar to get her way in most things," replied Cornelia.

Phyllis let out a loud laugh, "Remember the WI meeting right before the Christmas holidays when there was a discussion about who would be in charge of decorating the church? Mabel Jones who was the head of the Christmas committee and Doris Fleming, the head of the flower committee both lost out when Julia stood up and calmly announced that because she was so closely affiliated with the vicar and understood his likes and dislikes – as if he'd have the courage to argue with her – she would be the best person to head the church decorating. I can still see the sparks coming out of Doris' eyes," she chortled.

"That was an ugly scene. You could feel the anger and resentment in the room. And the worst part was that no one opposed her," said Debra with a slight shiver.

Phyllis, with a forkful loaded with minced lamb and mashed potatoes, dropped the fork and said, "And what about the nasty cat going over to the

Toadstool Book Shop to try to prohibit Debra's books from being sold there? Of course, the majority of mothers heard about that scheme and told the owner that if he stopped selling Debra's books, they would order not only their children's books but all their books on-line." Phyllis' anger showed in the rigid expression on her face.

Susana quickly jumped into the conversation. "Oh, I know she was tiresome, but..." and then she looked pensive and continued, "Well actually in the last few months every time I'd see her in the village, she'd find some way to let me know that she noticed I was putting on weight. Really, it got somewhat embarrassing because I never noticed it myself – my clothes size hasn't changed - she always managed to leave me feeling guilty. "Do I look fat to you?"

The others responded in unison. "Of course not, Susana! You know she was spiteful," was Debra's emphatic reply.

"You shouldn't let anything that old cat said bother you," said Phyllis.

Cornelia returned, "Susana, you've always been round but to say that you're continually putting on weight is ridiculous and only Julia would think to say that."

Debra shook her head sadly and said, "I used to feel so badly for the vicar. You know he'd love to come over to our house for dinner when Julia was away. I'm not..."

She didn't get a chance to finish her thought because Cornelia exclaimed, "Did you say away! Julia away? When was Julia away?"

"You didn't know?" cried Phyllis, "Well with you two flying back and forth across the pond you aren't privy to all the gossip. For the past year she's been going to London on a regular basis. About once a month or so and she's been staying overnight if that means anything!"

Cornelia sighed saying, "The vicar must have looked forward to those times. Imagine having someone continuously telling you how to behave, what to wear, what to eat and what to drink. Ugh, it makes me furious. No wonder he'd jump at the chance to go to your place. The poor guy was starved of not only food but also normal adult companionship."

Looking wistful, Debra replied, "He did enjoy the liquor we served. It seems that Julia allowed him to have only one teeny glass of sherry before dinner and wouldn't hear of serving any wine."

"Yeah, but the vicar's not a complete pushover, he delightedly told us he had a bottle hidden in his bathroom hamper. The housekeepers were always in collusion with him and would remove it if they thought Julia was going to search laundry!" Phyllis replied with obvious enjoyment.

Sergeant Rogers was successful in getting hold of Jim McCarthy who at that moment, owing to the minor detail of being the only full-time staff member on the paper and the fact that one of his part-time assistants had just broken a tooth at lunch and was at that moment sitting in a dentist's chair while the other assistant had been sick in bed with the flu for three days, was himself nursing a full blown migraine. He suspected the reason for the inspector's sudden request to see him and readily agreed to come down to the station eager for any excuse to leave the office and the mountain of work on his desk.

Upon entering the Inspector's office, Jim

McCarthy immediately apologized for any inconvenience that his story of that morning might have caused. "I realize that I might have stepped over the line with the suggestion that the issue of land played a part in the suspicious death of Julia Peters." Then leaning forward in his chair and looking and sounding more like a detective than the Inspector, he continued, "I might as well tell you that I have been doing a little investigating myself." Aware that both the inspector and sergeant exchanged looks, he added, "I am, after all, the managing editor of a newspaper and as it's leading investigative reporter it's my business to report the news."

The inspector reflected on this statement and although he agreed in theory, remembered that morning's conversation with his Chief Constable and decided he'd better correct the editor's perception of who was in charge of the investigation.

"I understand, of course that you must do your job as a reporter, Mr. McCarthy, but on the other hand I have to make it clear to you that any information which you might obtain must be cleared by us before you print it in your paper."

Inspector Bunson wondered for the umpteenth time how easy it was for reporters to get information from citizens whereas the police had to first present badges and documentation before anyone would even speak to them. Then turning his attention to documents on his desk he asked, "And in your 'investigations' sir, were you able to find out anything else we should know about?"

Again, the newspaperman leaned forward giving the impression that what he was about to say was not only interesting but extremely confidential. "That's just it Inspector. Julia Peters was not an esteemed person in the village. In fact I would go so far as to say that the residents of Epping looked upon her with fear."

The inspector squinted at his papers, nose twitching, and without looking up responded, "Well, thank you Mr. McCarthy, if that's all we..."

Jim McCarthy broke in before he was dismissed. "Inspector, I realize that you have good reason to be annoyed. But I took a risk – a risk which might prove useful in finding the person who murdered Julia Peters."

"And how do you think you're assumptions will allow us to find the murderer?" demanded the inspector.

"If you'll just let me finish Inspector. I'm more than happy to give you all the information at my disposal. All I ask is that you hear me out."

Inspector Bunson took the stack of papers he was perusing and pushed them over to one side and said, "Alright, we're listening."

The editor gave the inspector a nod of appreciation and began, "I know I should have mentioned what I'm about to tell you earlier but I've actually just remembered the conversation. You see, at the time I thought it was another one of Julia's self-important fantasies. This wouldn't be the first time she's come to me with bizarre innuendos. I listen politely and think about where I'll go fishing. Anyway, Julia disclosed to me the fact that the Leslie family were going to make a gift to the town of some land which abutted the cemetery. She was very secretive saying that the gift hadn't been made public yet. But now I'm not so sure. You see, she also hinted that there was another person who had been interested in purchasing this particular parcel from the Leslies. I remember thinking at the time that she seemed to be reveling in the fact that they 'lost out'." The editor looked embarrassed, "I know I should have come forward with this information sooner but this case has caused such a sensation that my stories are being picked up by the London papers!"

Inspector Bunson nodded thoughtfully then asked, "Why was all this disclosed to you Mr. McCarthy? Were you a close friend of the deceased?"

For the first time that morning the editor looked amused and gave a hearty laugh. "Julia had no friends Inspector - at least none that I ever noticed. She had an annoying habit of coming to our office every Thursday morning to give us her outline for 'The Village News' section of the paper. We initially agreed to *one* column when she first approached us to 'suggest' the section. This column has steadily grown into *three*! Mainly information about all the good she's doing and how she's doing it. My two assistants have renamed that section "Julia's Detractions".

A snicker came from the corner of the room and then Sergeant Rogers could be heard coughing loudly.

The inspector tried to regain the dignity of his office by asking, "Mr. McCarthy do you think that Ms. Peters could have given anyone else the same information she gave you?"

Jim McCarthy looked earnestly at Inspector Bunson and said, "You know Inspector, I've been wondering about that myself. As I said earlier, anyone will tell you that Julia's main objective in life was to reign over the village of Epping. It was common knowledge that she adored shocking people with scuttlebutt or hearsay – very successfully, I might add. What I'm trying to say, Inspector is that she very well might have said something to multiple people."

After escorting the newspaperman to the door with a reminder that any and all information obtained had to be reviewed by Scotland Yard prior to being printed, Sergeant Rogers returned to the office where he found his superior standing in front of the window.

"Disliking Julia seems to be a universal sentiment," commented the Inspector still facing the window.

"Inspector, when Jim said that bit about Julia telling him that 'someone else' had been interested in buying that piece of land why didn't you ask him who that person is?"

Inspector Bunson turned to look at his Sergeant and replied, "Think about it, Sergeant, what other person has land that abuts the Leslies?"

Chapter 15

After a delicious lunch followed by even better desserts, the four women made their way out of the teashop. Before getting to the door, Susana decided it would be a good idea to buy some '*Maids of Honor*' to take home for tea. Following Susana's example, Debra also took advantage of buying a few pastries that she had passed up at dessert.

"Really, I could order the entire display! I can't decide which to take," she said as she tried to make up her mind.

"Well then why don't you take one of each and freeze them?" suggested Susana laughing.

Unable to guess whether or not Susana was serious, Debra replied, "Don't tempt me, I think I'll just take a dozen of the double chocolate cookies and another dozen of the raspberry bars."

Once outside, Phyllis exclaimed at the sight of the bags of pastries Debra was carrying and in her good-natured way declared that the bicycle ride they had planned would now have to be shortened.

The women parted company just as the Inspector and his Sergeant were crossing the street headed for the Ravens Roost.

"Good afternoon ladies. This is a pleasant coincidence," greeted Inspector Bunson.

"Oh indeed Inspector, and of course Mikey, we are always delighted to see you! Aren't we Cornelia?" replied Susana somewhat apprehensively.

Inspector Bunson smiled, "Very kind of you, I'm sure. We were planning on paying a call at your home later this afternoon regarding a small matter in our investigation."

Noting the startled look on Susana's face, the Inspector quickly added, "Nothing to worry about. We need some clarification on whether you or your brother told anyone aside from the Reverend Peters, about the donation of land prior to the dinner party."

Cornelia looked questioningly at Susana. It was common knowledge that Susana was entirely guileless and unable to control her mouth. And on more than one occasion it was these traits that landed her in some very precarious situations.

Susana, cognizant of the thoughts passing through her sister's mind, immediately shook her head and blinking furiously replied, "Not one word, Inspector. I really never thought that donating a piece of land that we never use was at all that important or significant. After all, it's not like we were giving away the Aga stove is it?"

The inspector and sergeant smiled politely. "Yes, I understand, but did anyone ask you about the land or donation in conversation?" continued Inspector Bunson hoping that this line of thought would jar something in Susana's memory.

"Inspector my sister and I were aboard ship on a cruise for most of a month. We of course were in communication with our brother and our attorney about the gift but we really had no need to let anyone else know about our family affairs." returned Cornelia.

The inspector decided that he had gotten as far as he was able with this line of questioning and to continue would result in less than favorable circumstances. He thanked the sisters for their time and walked off with his Sergeant for much needed refreshment.

"Oh Cornelia, this whole thing is getting on my nerves. I never would have thought that a silly thing like a piece of land would have the whole village and town in such an uproar. Much less a...murder! Did you?" asked Susana as she watched the policemen walk away.

"I wouldn't get too upset, Susana, I'm sure it'll all get sorted out," replied Cornelia trying to sound convincing.

"Hmm, somehow I'm not so sure," returned a thoughtful Susana. Then in an about face of mood she continued, "Cornelia, why don't we go into Madame Sonia's? I noticed that they have her winter collection already displayed in the windows and some new clothes might help calm my nerves. Don't you think?"

The sisters happily made their way towards the village's premier ladies' fashion boutique owned and run by a heavily made up Argentine fashion maven who no matter what time of day it was could always be counted on to wear shimmering sequins.

After a lunch which felt as though it bared as little thinking about as possible, Inspector Bunson turned his thoughts to the chairman of the town's selectmen.

"If you can manage to lumber, much less walk, after that gargantuan meal, we can pay a visit to Sam Taylor," he teased his Sergeant not without envy.

Sergeant Rogers, with a sigh of contentment, answered, "Yeah, I really think the best food is found in pubs. Can't beat a pub for real English food made just like mum's – actually better. By the way, you should have tried the steak and kidney pudding, melted in your mouth!"

With a sidelong glance of astonishment, the Inspector replied, "I value my hands to highly to venture them anywhere near your plate when you're chowing down. And besides, you finished so quickly it was all I could do to keep your fork out of my plate! Actually, I owe you a debt of gratitude for finishing that huge serving of fish and chips."

"That's just it sir, not only is pub food good, the servings are generous and they don't gauge your wallet. Unlike that nouvelle cuisine fiddle-daddle that looks like a preschooler made out of play dough and tastes like it too. You get two forkfuls and you're out of food – and money!" said an impassioned Rogers.

The village of Epping, was set in a valley surrounded by hills. Sam Taylor's farm was situated on a knoll overlooking the village and the surrounding woods.

Sergeant Rogers drove the police car along the scenic winding road, bordered by village homes and woods. Before the car took the turn onto a dirt driveway the sound of a tractor along with the sweet smell of newly cut hay drifted into the car. About fifty yards along they came to a small building which contained only three sides. A long trestle table ran the length of the inside of the building and on one end of the table were stacked pumpkins of all shapes, sizes and colors, the center of the table was covered with the last of the summer's crop of tomatoes, green beans and squash and at the end were buckets of chrysanthemums in shades of gold, burgundy, white and yellow. Lastly, a small table held the few remaining jars of the summer's strawberries, raspberries, boysenberries, quince and gooseberries made into preserves. A sign by each of the items gave their price. As is typical in the country, the honor system had long been a custom regarding payment with a small wooden box with a removable lid holding the day's proceeds.

Although the officers could hear the sound of the tractor and the general direction from which it came, the large shrubs bordering the drive made it impossible to see beyond the white fencing. They continued driving and soon came upon a large expanse of open land again bordered by white fencing and graceful willows. About five hundred yards ahead they could see a long white building with a red roof and a rotunda in the center. In the rotunda stood huge open double doors.

As the car got nearer the building, the officers discerned the unmistakable odor of horses. Sure enough, as they approached the circular drive, a man walking beside a horse could be seen entering the double doors. Sergeant Rogers parked the car and both men followed the other into the stables. The air was filled with the scent of horse, old leather, tanning oils, hay, and saddle soap. To Inspector Bunson, who had been raised in the city, this was undoubtedly the finest equestrian structure he had ever seen. Upon entering, they found themselves in a circular arena lit by windows high up in the rotunda. Flanking the rotunda were two wings of stables that housed a minimum of ten horses each. From the wing to their right closest to the entrance they could hear voices.

As they headed in the direction of the voices, they came upon the man they had seen walking the horse. He was outside a stall brushing down the animal. Sergeant Rogers asked where they might find Sam Taylor. The man pointed to the tack room saying, "Tom will call him for you. That's him you hear out ploughing the south field."

Inspector Bunson decided that this would be a good opportunity to walk around the farm and said that they would meet Sam out on the field. They were given directions and by walking through a golden field of yarrow they were able to locate the farmer standing by an outbuilding with a corrugated tin roof used as a type of garage for farm equipment.

Sam was at a sink in the garage washing his hands and face. When he heard the police officers he turned around and grabbing a towel that was hanging by the sink apologized for the dust that clung to his clothes.

"Ploughing is a dirty business even if you're atop a tractor!" he continued to explain, "October's when we have to turn over the ground and furrow for the next crop." "It certainly is peaceful here," replied the Inspector looking around. As if on cue, loud lowing was heard immediately behind them. The Inspector quickly turned to look and saw a herd of cattle appearing just over a small incline in the field across from where they stood.

The farmer gave an amused smile and said, "Those'll be my Jersey's. This is partly a dairy farm, you know."

"Ah," remarked the Inspector somewhat self-consciously. In the manner of persons city born and bred, he was inclined to have a romantic view of agricultural life.

Sergeant Rogers picked up the slack, "We came in by the stables, I wanted to show the inspector that amazing building. Are you still giving riding lessons?"

"Yep, we have a couple of instructors but lately what with the depressed economy students have been having to drop out."

"Didn't you also have polo matches out on your field there? I remember seeing a match when I was a kid."

The farmer's eyes lit up and with a sheepish grin he said, "That's what I live for. Nothing fancy – don't go in for that stuff. We just have the locals with horses come up once a month for a match. Every June we have a charity exhibition with professional polo players which brings out a good crowd. That's a real treat."

"That's a lot of horses you keep," remarked the inspector. He wondered at the expense such an operation incurred.

Astutely guessing the reason behind the Inspector's question the farmer answered, "Oh, I only have four of my own. I mostly rent the stalls out – we have some nice trails in this part of the country – although a lot of folks are having to sell off their horses. In my grandfather's time this was a stud farm but it got to be so expensive that when my father took over the farm he decided to go primarily dairy. Of course we produce our own feed for the animals along with the crops which we grow for commercial distribution."

Inspector Bunson seemed to forget the reason behind his visit to Sam Taylor. He was awestruck by the idyllic beauty of the place and he wondered if the hard life of farming wasn't compensated by the unequalled beauty of the land. He was brought back to the present by a sharp, piercing pain in his neck. Then immediately he felt a hard slap.

"Inspector you're not allergic to wasps are you?" asked his worried Sergeant trying to wipe his superior's neck with a handkerchief.

"Not that I know of," answered a momentarily stunned inspector. Then regaining his composure replied, "And stop poking at me with that filthy rag."

Ignoring his chief's remark, Sergeant Rogers replied, "Actually I just took it out of my drawer this morning. But if you want to wear a dead wasp on your neck that's okay by me."

Inspector Bunson quickly pulled out his own handkerchief and wiped the painful spot which by now had blossomed into a painful node. Then, to his credit, with as much dignity as possible, turned to the farmer and said, "Mr. Taylor, I don't want to take up any more of your valuable time, I can see you have plenty to do. It's come to our attention that you were interested in buying the land that the Leslie family donated to the town. Is that true?"

"Inspector, that's public knowledge. I actually brought that up before the Ways and Means Committee about three months ago."

"I don't quite understand Mr. Taylor. What business was it of the town's if you wanted to purchase a piece of land? Also, three months ago, no one knew that the family had any intention of parting with that bit of land. Or did they?"

The farmer continued calmly, "I guess I didn't Explain myself clearly, Inspector, the business I brought up before the committee had to do with the issue of commercial development. And yes, I was surprised when I learned that that parcel was being considered as a donation. Now that I come to think of it, it was Julia who told me."

"Did you have discussions about this with her?" asked the Inspector. He wondered how much capital it would take to run a small farm much less something of this size.

"No, but I believe I had mentioned that I was thinking of expanding the farm."

Inspector Bunson gave Sam a questioning look and asked, "In what context did that topic come up in conversation?"

Sam's eyes crinkled in the handsome, weathered face and he broke into a lopsided grin, "Inspector, if you haven't already found out, there are no secrets in a village." Then with one last brush at his pants he pointed in the direction of the cows and said, "If that's all you gentlemen have come about, I'd like to check the feeders."

"Don't the cows just graze in the pasture?" asked the inspector looking around for visible containers.

Lifting himself over the fence, Sam replied, "Yes and no. Dairy cows need specialized nutrition. We give them specially prepared feed in the barn so they get all the nutrients while at the same time producing the best possible milk. We have a bunch of young male cattle called feeders and which we sell as beef cattle." From the other side of the fence he continued, "Would you like to come and take a look?" The cows began to meander towards Sam until he was practically surrounded by Jerseys.

Sergeant Rogers would have happily climbed over but for the Inspector's prompt reply that there was considerable paperwork waiting for them at the station.

A disappointed sergeant had to quicken his pace to catch up with his Inspector. "What paperwork do we have, Inspector? Is there a new development that I'm not aware of?" he asked trying to keep a straight face.

"Not 'we' Sergeant, you," replied the Inspector slowing down. "I want you to check up on the Taylor estate. It wouldn't surprise me to find that running a place like this costs a mint. Then looking around he continued, "I'd be interested to know if Sam Taylor operates at a profit or a loss."

Chapter 16

By mid afternoon, the sisters were on their way back to the house and Susana was looking forward to tea.

"I just adore Madame Sonia. She has so much style and an uncanny ability to know what will look good on me. That skirt and jacket set will be perfect for the cold months ahead. Do you think she'll have it ready in a week's time?" she chattered happily as they continued their walk home.

"She definitely knows what she's doing. The tailoring and material are always of the best quality but why does she insist on wearing all that glitter and her make-up looks like she's about to step onto the stage," replied Cornelia as they passed the woods known as 'Hunter's Bosk' just east of the village.

"Oh I don't know, I think as a fashionista she needs to be a little over the top. Don't you think?" replied Susana wiping her forehead with a handkerchief. Then, casting a side-long glance towards the woods, she continued, "Oh it does look inviting in the nice shade. I'm almost tempted to sit under one of those oaks to catch my breath. Aren't you...well for heaven's sake...who's that?"

Susana's sentence was left hanging as she noticed a figure coming out of the woods running at a fast clip. The sisters stood frozen and speechless staring at the individual who was heading in their direction. As it got closer the sisters were able to discern the figure of a female in a flowing skirt, long, skinny legs that leaped more than ran and long skinny arms flailing in every direction. The mad expression on the face and the unkempt red hair clinched the identity of the person.

"Oh, my gosh, it's Martha!" exclaimed Susana and Cornelia in unison as they quickly stepped onto the grassy verge to avoid Martha's buffeting limbs.

"Martha, what's wrong?" shouted Cornelia as Martha got to within twenty feet. Martha continued her vaulting run without slowing down. It was as if she couldn't see the two women she was about to pass by and every couple of seconds, a gasp would escape from her mouth.

"Martha, what's the matter? Is someone after you?" asked a frightened Susana addressing Martha's back as the woman continued her frenzied dash from the woods.

Susana quickly grabbed her sister's arm and with a frightened look in the direction of the woods, said, "We'd better hurry home, our tea will be getting cold – do you think she's running away from someone…or *something*?"

With the onset of autumn, it was getting dark earlier and the sisters quickened their pace towards the manor. At one point, as they came over a slight incline, they caught a glimpse of a head of unruly hair bobbing along the winding footpath below them.

"That's odd, looks like Martha's heading towards Blandings," murmured Cornelia.

"She looked like she was scared out of her wits, Cornelia," said Susana, then immediately added,

"Oh, but she doesn't have any wits, does she?"

"She definitely seemed more wacky than usual. Now don't start getting worked up, Susana, we all know that Martha's behavior is always erratic and histrionic. She probably got into a fight with her sister or any one of her nutty relatives and is acting out accordingly."

By this time the sisters had arrived at the manor and were taking off their wraps in the front hall. "I'm going to look for Martha in the kitchen. I wonder if Jack's home?" said Susana rushing towards the back hall with Cornelia right behind her. In the kitchen the sisters found an agitated Pinkey.

"I'm sorry tea's going to take a bit longer. Auntie Martha practically broke the kitchen door down trying to get in just now. And when I finally opened it she wouldn't answer me when I asked if she'd lost her key. She's in such a state that there's nothing I can do to calm her down. Keeps shrieking, crying and babbling all at the same time. I don't know what's gotten in her!"

"So she's back for good?" asked a bewildered Susana.

"I don't know M'am, she showed up later than usual around two o'clock and kept me running around with instructions on how to cook the dinner!" She changed her tone from exasperation to pride and continued, "I hope you don't mind, Mrs. S., I found a nice foreign recipe in your books for potatoes – it's called 'Oh Great Tin Potatoes'– I'm sure I've never seen potatoes look so good as in the photo in your book."

Momentarily forgetting about Martha, Susana answered, "I'm sure they'll turn out even better than in the photo Pinky and of course you can use the cookbooks any time you like, that's what they're there for. Isn't that right Cornelia?"

There was no answer from Cornelia because at that moment she was patiently but deliberately asking that Martha open her bedroom door.

From inside Martha's room could be heard low moaning sounds followed by wailing noises. Cornelia added to the ruckus by persistent pounding on the door.

Hearing the commotion, Susana ran out of the kitchen and down the hall towards the noise with Pinky close on her heels. "Cornelia what is going on here?" she asked out of breath.

Pinky remained behind Susana her hands wringing her apron. "I forgot to tell you, when Martha burst in she ran through the first floor closing all the windows and making sure that all the doors were locked then she ran into her room and slammed the door in my face. She fair looked barmy."

"Pinky, go and get Mr. Jack please. Don't you think someone should break down the door Cornelia?" asked Susana almost in tears.

"Mr. Jack went to town on business Mrs. S. He told me he had already told you not to hold dinner for him as he didn't know what time he'd get home," replied Pinky her voice quavering.

Seeing the alarm on Pinkey's face Susana quickly said, "I'm sure Martha's going to be fine – she probably only has a headache. Everything will be fine. Is that clear?"

"Oh, it's not Martha I'm worried about, she's just acting her old self – it's the dinner I'm thinking about. I don't want the 'Oh Great Tin Potatoes' to burn!"

Cornelia pushed past them saying she was

going to get the main set of keys. She returned a little while later carrying several keys on a satin rope. "Let's hope one of these will open this door," she said as she tried the first key. It took several exasperating attempts before the right key slid smoothly into the lock. A second later, the sound of a key hitting the floor could be heard on the opposite side of the door.

Both sisters held their breath in trepidation before opening the door. Once entering, Susana picked up the fallen key and placed it on the bureau. They found Martha lying down on the bed with the covers pulled completely over her head. She was still moaning and every once in a while her legs made a motion that made it look like she was pedaling a bicycle.

Standing behind her sister and peering fearfully at Martha Susana whispered, "Should we call Dr. Goodman?"

"I don't know yet. Maybe if we give her some sherry she'll calm down. Pinkey would you mind getting a glass of sherry for your aunt?"

Pinkey immediately ran out of the room and brought back a glass filled to the brim with sherry. Handing the glass to Cornelia she pointed to the pocket of her apron and said, "I brought the bottle just in case she needs more."

Cornelia approached the side of the bed with the glass of sherry and proceeded to try to pull the covers off of Martha resulting in half of the sherry spilling on top of Martha's head. Martha promptly sat up howling incomprehensible protestations and holding the covers up to her face. Her eyes skimmed the entire room with a demented stare. Cornelia held out the remaining sherry imploring her to drink it.

With shaking hands, Martha grabbed the glass

and finished the contents with one swig. Then after wiping her mouth with the covers looked at the three people in the room and declared, "I'm not leavin' this room and you can't make me. I'm stayin' right 'ere with the door locked – 'ow did you get in 'ere anyhow?" She didn't wait for an answer resuming her caterwauling with a demented look on her face.

Susana, who had remained speechless and afraid of doing anything that might make things worse, hastily suggested that Pinky pour Martha another glass of sherry.

Pinky, who was quite used to Martha's bizarre conduct, took it all in stride and walking up to Martha, picked up the glass and began to pour the sherry. With amazing agility, Martha snatched the bottle from Pinkey and began to drink from the bottle gulping loudly. Pausing only when an errant swallow caused a coughing fit.

The sisters kept their distance mesmerized by the spectacle. Presently the effects of the sherry took hold and Martha's demeanor changed to continual rocking back and forth all the while keeping a tight hold on the bottle of sherry with intermittent cries that all doors and windows be kept locked.

"I think we can safely leave her now. With the amount of alcohol that she's consumed it won't be long before she's sound asleep," said Cornelia ushering the other two women out the door.

"Ooo, I don't know about that," replied Pinkey shaking her head, "Auntie Martha can out drink most of the men in the village. She holds the record over at the Raven's Roost for the most shots of tequila in ten seconds!"

"Did she pass out?" asked Susana fascinated.

Pinkey laughed, "Nope, she stayed bright as

day until closing. Of course she was out cold for twenty-four hours when she finally went to bed. But she never even had a headache when she finally got up!"

Susana's jaw dropped. "There's no end of surprises where Martha's concerned. Is there?"

"So who's surprised?" was Cornelia's glib reply.

Chapter 17

"How many slices of pizza have you consumed?" asked an incredulous Inspector Bunson looking at two empty pizza boxes.

"Hey, if you're not going to eat them somebody has to. Besides, I need all the nourishment I can get if I'm going to work a sixteen-hour day," replied Sergeant Rogers happily munching while staring at his computer screen.

Opening up the third box as if it contained a toxic substance, the Inspector examined the contents. Tasting a small piece of sausage to make sure that it was indeed edible, he removed a slice of pizza and was surprised at how good it tasted. Quietly finishing his second slice he said, "This isn't bad. What's in it?"

Eyes fixated on his computer screen, Rogers answered, "That's their best seller. They call it *'Everything But the Kitchen Sink'*. I ordered two of those."

Without saying a word, the Inspector opened the top drawer of his desk, opened a plastic bottle and swallowed his trusty tablets.

"So now that my brilliant computer skills have discovered that Sam Taylor's property is mortgaged to the hilt what are we going to do about it?" asked

Sergeant Rogers.

"We'll go see farmer Taylor in the morning and ask him for an explanation. But for now I think we can call it a night," answered the inspector putting on his coat.

A knock at the door brought a constable into the room with news that a body had just been found in Hunter's Bosk.

I'll go get the car. Meet you out in front," said Rogers grabbing his coat.

Almost immediately the inspector's phone rang. It was the Chief Constable with more information and a request that the Inspector take over the investigation.

Getting into the police car, Inspector Bunson relayed the information to his sergeant, "Don't rush, Betty Smith is in the hospital with severe head trauma. The doctors aren't sure if she'll survive. Two kids in their early twenties found her in the woods tonight and called emergency services.

They're with Dibbs and Jenkins at the scene." Sergeant Rogers thought the inspector looked as if he had aged ten years since dinner.

When they arrived at Hunter's Bosk, Constable Jenkins was eagerly awaiting them. As the officers approached, he pulled at the overly snug uniform jacket and stood at wobbly attention until the Inspector motioned him to relax.

"So where'd it happen?" asked Sergeant Rogers looking around for the customary yellow tape.

"Just inside the grove of rhodies over this way, Sir. Constable Dibbs is keeping watch over the two who notified us." Constable Jenkins lead the officers off the path towards a grove of native rhododendrons all the while pinching himself over the fact that he was actually in the midst of another homicide, well, almost a homicide. He could hardly believe his luck. In his excitement, large beads of perspiration dribbled from under his helmet as he ambled ahead of the Scotland Yard men.

About fifty feet from the path, well covered by huge oak trees and luxurious native shrubs they came upon a luxuriant grove of rhododendrons surrounded by yellow tape. An elderly constable was standing with his back to the approaching policemen, talking to two people seated on a rock. On hearing Constable Jenkins' labored breathing, he turned around and gave a quick salute to the men from Scotland Yard. Not wanting to pass up his big opportunity, Constable Jenkins hurriedly stepped in front of his fellow constable and trying his best to sound like the police detective on his favorite television show, pointed to an area that had evidence of soil being disturbed. Realizing that he actually had the attention of the officers he went into full acting mode, pulled out his notepad, mimicked the fictional detective and continued, "I've taken down their information and made sure that nothing has been disturbed." Neither Inspector Bunson nor Officer Rogers failed to hear the snort that came from the direction of Constable Dibbs.

Inspector Bunson purposely refrained from looking at his Sergeant and replied, "Thanks Constable, we can talk to them a little later – oh, we'll go over your notes then. The rest of the CSI team were right behind us so they should be here presently. Would you mind looking out for them?"

With Constable Jenkins out of the way, the Inspector and Sergeant directed their attention to the spot where Betty Smith had been found. Sergeant

Rogers called to Constable Dibbs to join them. "Is their story credible? Didn't touch anything?" he asked looking in the direction of the kids.

Constable Dibbs, true to his countryman's breed, and having known Rogers since birth, screwed his eyes up at him, sniffed and with his native penchant for eloquence, said, "Couple kids out neckin' - don't you know these woods' been used by kids since the year one? Didn't go near the poor girl, just called 999."

"Yeah, okay Charlie," replied Sergeant Rogers having grown up with Dibbs as the village constable. "Were you here when the ambulance arrived?"

Constable Dibbs spat to show his disgust. "'Course I was. I was the first one on the scene even if that fool Billy Jenkins acts like he was a cop on one of those TV shows. He actually makes workin' with him entertainin'!" and with that, Constable Dibbs spat again in an attempt to put emphasis on this last statement.

"You didn't let him trample on anything did you?" asked an anxious Rogers.

Constable Dibbs, using his advanced age and time on the force to an advantage, gave Rogers a look of dismay and this time let out a snort that was impossible to ignore.

From the direction of the path, Constable Jenkins' audible wheezing announced the arrival of the CSI team.

Sergeant Rogers, after politely glancing at the constable's notes, walked over to the two young people who sat watching the activity in holy terror and in his most casual manner asked them to go over their story. This done, he walked back to the inspector who had been giving instructions to the team.

"Nothing useful. The kids didn't see anything or anyone but they got a nasty surprise when they found Ms. Smith. Didn't know if she was alive or dead. But they knew not to touch anything – thanks to Hollywood. Betty Smith is lucky those kids were around when they were."

In the inky darkness of the evening, Inspector Bunson looked around the tranquil and secluded wood and nodded in agreement.

As the inspector and his sergeant made their way out of the woods and headed back to the path, they could hear voices coming from the entrance to Hunter's Bosk. As they approached closer to the sounds they could discern the voice of Constable Jenkins and that of a female carrying on a very animated discussion. Once on the path and with their flashlights focused in the direction of the voices, Sergeant Rogers was able to recognize Pinkey.

"The girl speaking to Jenkins is another Jenkins," Rogers informed the inspector, then lowering his voice he continued, "She's actually an oddity in that family because she's the only normal member."

Upon seeing Sergeant Rogers, Pinkey turned bright red and stared down at her shoes.

"Hello Pinkey, isn't it a bit late for you to be out in these parts?" asked Rogers smiling.

Looking up shyly and seeing the sergeant's friendly face, Pinkey regained her composure. "Well you see I should have been home an hour ago but there was ever a lot to do what with Auntie Martha having fits and shutting herself up in her room shrieking something awful. When it quieted down I decided a good walk would help to clear my head of all the ruckus Auntie made. I had to dodge Mrs. S. on account of her insisting that Mr. Jack accompany me."

"Heck, I thought she weren't sleepin' in the big 'ouse no more. I knew 'er and yur ma couldn't stick it out under one roof. They be pullin' each other's 'air since they were tiny mites," chimed in Constable Jenkins with little professionalism.

Although her uncle's facts were correct, Pinkey spoke up in defense of her mother, "You've no right to go speaking about your own flesh and blood like that, Uncle Billy. You know Ma and Auntie Martha have good times together. It's Auntie's moods that get her in trouble. She doesn't know if she's happy or angry from one minute to the next! And if you must know, she's still staying at our place. In fact she left the manor headed for home at five o'clock today on account of it getting dark so early now."

"Then what's she doin' back at the big 'ouse and locked up in 'er old room, Missy?" asked the constable once more forgetting that his senior officers were beside him.

Having listened to enough of the Jenkins' family tribulations, the Inspector and Sergeant were about to say good night and allow the two participants to resolve their family issues without an audience when they were stopped cold by Pinkey's response to her uncle.

"Well, Mr. Smarty, why don't you go and ask the Mrs. Leslies? They saw Auntie running out of the woods like she was bonkers and heading right back to the big house!"

"What did you just say?" asked the inspector

151

looking at the girl with interest.

"Are you talking about Martha?" inquired the Sergeant.

Constable Jenkins, with startling cognizance heretofore unseen, became aware that his niece might have some pertinent information regarding the assault on Betty and demanded, "Well? Don't just stand there pertendin' to be a mute. Answer the men!"

Pinkey looked from one to the other with wide, searching eyes.

Sergeant Rogers came to the rescue. "No need to be frightened Pinkey, you didn't say anything wrong. It's just that there was an accident in Hunter's Bosk earlier today and we're trying to figure out what happened. If, as you say, your Aunt Martha came out of those woods she might have seen something that might help us find the cause of the accident," he finished with what he hoped was an encouraging smile.

The sergeant's charm once again had its intended effect. Pinkey returned his smile, "I don't know if Auntie saw anything. She hasn't really said anything logical since she came barreling into the manor."

"Oh jeez," escaped from the constable.

The two officers exchanged glances. "We'll go over to the manor now and speak to your aunt. But first we'll drive you home," said Inspector Bunson.

"Oh, thanks, that'd be great. I really don't like walking through the woods when it's this dark. But I think you'll be wasting your time going to speak with Auntie. She's been locked up in her room acting like a scared rabbit," answered Pinkey.

Chapter 18

With Pinkey delivered safely home, the two officers headed for the manor with Sergeant Rogers behind the wheel.

"So we have three possible witnesses to the assault," he said as he maneuvered the car through the village.

"I was wondering if you had picked up...good gracious! Can't you slow down when you go around those curves?" blasted the Inspector reaching for the dashboard, while pressing down on invisible brakes.

"Oh, sorry. I learned to drive on these roads – I bet I could drive them blindfolded. But yeah, of course I picked up on Pinkey's story that the Mrs. Leslies saw Martha come out of the woods. Hey, you don't think they had anything to do with Betty's assault do you? I mean, it'd be completely out of character for them to do anything like that."

The inspector gave a grim laugh and said, "I agree that they don't look like cold-blooded murderers but we can't rule them out based on looks or past behavior, more's the pity," then with an exasperated tone he continued, "What's taking so long with the background checks anyway? We should have gotten them by now."

With overt slowing of the car around a sharp

154

curve, Sergeant Rogers, exclaimed, "Oh gosh, I was waiting until we got back to the car to tell you. Thanks for reminding me."

"Tell me what?" asked a weary Inspector digging into his pockets for the bottle of tablets. He was trying to ignore a niggling notion that he'd have better luck solving a homicide in the City than in this place where everyone, including the constables, seemed to have been either just released or escaped from the looney bin.

"That as I was going to get the car earlier tonight, Sergeant Matthews handed me the report. It's there in the back seat inside my briefcase."

"And to think that just a couple of hours ago I was putting on my coat, looking forward to a peaceful evening at home," sighed the Inspector in reply.

At eleven o'clock that evening, the inspector and sergeant pulled up to Blandings. Susana Leslie opened the door. By the anxious expression on her face it was immediately evident that something was not quite right in the household.

"Oh Inspector and Mikey, I mean Sergeant Rogers. Are you here to help with Martha? Really, she's been so trying – more so than usual. I can't imagine what's gotten into her, really I can't. But now that you're here everything should be fine. Shouldn't it?"

Jack Leslie came out of the library, "Good evening gentlemen. Are you here to see Martha? Unlike Susana, I don't think you need bother with Martha's histrionics. She has some sort of episode on a weekly basis. But if you insist on seeing her, first come into the library for a quick pick me up and believe me, you'll need it if you're planning to question her."

"Very kind of you Mr. Leslie. We actually were hoping to have a few words with you and your sisters about your activities earlier this evening. As for your kind offer, much as we'd like, we'll have to decline," replied the inspector following Jack into the library.

"You see Jack," began his sister, it's a good thing you didn't stay in London." Then turning to the officers continued, "Well then I'll just go and find Cornelia. She was in the mudroom cleaning off our walking shoes. So much mud in the country don't you agree?"

Jack shook his head as he mixed himself a cocktail, "Why my sisters insist on keeping Martha employed here is a mystery to me. Sure I can't offer you anything from the bar?"

"I'm good, thanks," replied Sergeant Rogers. "Could you tell us why you went up to London?"

After taking a long sip of his cocktail Jack answered, "Surely. Let's see, I left here right after breakfast and headed straight for my broker's – Alfred Singleton of Singleton and Co. I arrived there about noonish, we went over some papers and then he took me to lunch to a new place with a designer menu. Believe me, you know you're in trouble when every other word in the menu is foreign and/or a food which you've never heard of much less tasted."

"Were you in London all day?" asked Rogers in his most casual manner. He was still getting used to having to ask people whom he had known all his life intrusive questions.

Jack gave them a quizzical look, "Most of the day. After lunch I decided that as long as I was in the City I'd check out the new exhibit at the Albert Museum. I'm a sucker for the military themed exhibits. After that I walked around Bond Street for a while and by tea time I was heading back here."

"And when did you purchase your museum ticket?" asked the inspector.

"That morning, on-line, of course. Much the easiest way these days - don't have to stand in line, you know. And if you're interested in what time I was home, I can tell you precisely because as I came in, Cornelia and Susana were standing by the kitchen door pleading unsuccessfully with Pinkey not to walk home at that hour – eight o'clock. A sentiment with which I concurred. By the way, why am I being asked about today? The murder took place three days ago!"

"Oh Jack, do you have to use that horrible word? Why can't you just say *'accident'*. I mean no one really knows for sure that Julia's death wasn't an allergic reaction to something," remarked Susana entering the room with Cornelia in tow. Then turning with a hopeful glance to the police officers, she added, "Isn't that right?"

Cornelia quickly spoke up. "Please don't feel you have to answer that. Susana is being capricious and unreasonable. We all know that someone killed Julia by poisoning her. Unfortunately, the murderer had the audacity to do it during a dinner party in our home."

Susana, looking at her siblings with reproach, walked over to an armchair in front of the fire and picking up a throw which lay neatly folded nearby carefully wrapped herself in it as if to shield herself from the ugly facts and stared into the fire with quiet dignity.

The inspector, feeling that he had somehow been scolded, fumbled with his hat, cleared his throat and announced, "It seems that there was another accident sometime this evening in Hunter's Bosk."

The sisters let out little screams simultaneously. Jack, the color having drained from his face, got up from the sofa and again made his way to the bar. It wasn't difficult to observe that his gait was more than a little unsteady. Pouring himself another cocktail, he asked, "By '*accident*' do you mean Susana's definition of accident or a homicide?"

"Betty Smith was found unconscious last night in Hunter's Bosk with a severe blow to the head. She's in the hospital and hasn't regained consciousness," pronounced Sergeant Rogers.

There was a sound of shattering glass followed by a few well-chosen words. Susana quickly jumped out of her chair and made her way across the room making clucking noises. "Now let me see your hand dear, I'll just go and get the first aid kit from the kitchen. Just keep your hand in the ice bucket. Does it hurt?" Still clucking she left the room.

"I don't know how I managed to do that. Careless of me," expressed Jack looking uncomfortably nervous as he attempted to make another cocktail.

"Better keep your hand in the ice," suggested Officer Rogers picking up the mixers and preparing a drink. Handing Jack the cocktail he added, "Did anyone accompany you to London?"

"If you're asking me if I went up to London with Betty, the answer is definitely not."

"Did you go with anyone else then?" asked the Inspector.

"No, the purpose of my trip was business not pleasure. You're more than welcome to check my movements with my broker." Thinking this over he continued, "I stayed in town after the meeting because of the infernal traffic on the roads. I thought I'd wait until the tea hour when there's less activity. As it was, I made it home in time for dinner."

Cornelia picked up where Jack left off, "That's right, Jack arrived home around eight o'clockish just in time to drive Pinkey home. Of course the silly girl refused the ride. In fact when you said there'd been an accident I could have sworn you were going to tell us that Pinkey was the victim. There's very little crime in this part of the world…er…that is, until now."

Susana burst into the room carrying a square, wooden box and rushed to attend to her brother saying, "Here you are Jack, I've brought everything I need to take care of your hand. Good boy, you've kept it in the ice." She proceeded to meticulously administer to Jack's wound.

Meanwhile, Inspector Bunson, who had an aberrant - considering his profession - aversion to blood kept his eyes scrupulously focused on the ceiling.

Having finished, with great enthusiasm - if little aptitude - the wrapping of her brother's hand so that it very nearly resembled a baseball catcher's mitt, Susana continued her monologue. "It's a good thing Martha's locked herself up in her room again. I can't think what she'd do if she saw all this blood!" Casually stuffing the implements of her labors into the wooden box, she continued, "Well, now that that's taken care of, what were you saying Mikey?"

Sergeant Rogers, contemplating a change of name, hastily replied, "Um, speaking of Martha, can you confirm that you and Ms. Cornelia saw her near Hunter's Bosk this evening?"

The sisters glanced at each other in

astonishment. "Yes, of course," they said in unison.

"I knew it. It was bound to happen sometime," declared Cornelia with a sigh.

Managing to hold back a chuckle, and hoping the Inspector hadn't seen his grin, the Sergeant began to type on his laptop. Before the inspector could ask what Cornelia meant by her statement, Susana chimed in.

"It is a pity about Martha. Of course the entire Jenkins family have always been unbalanced and Martha's no exception - nutty as a fruitcake. I've dreaded the day the authorities would take her away. And now it's happened. Isn't that why you're here?"

Wondering if it wasn't too late to put in his application for retirement, Inspector Bunson, replied, "W-e-l l-l yes and no."

Jack, who had been quietly sipping his fourth cocktail of the evening, interjected and with a slight slur said, "Let me help you out Inspector." Turning to his sisters he continued, "Girls, the Inspector and Mike are here because you were seen earlier in the day near Hunter's Bosk where evidently some lunatic coshed Betty over the head. In their capacity as officers of the law they're here to grill you...er...us as to our whereabouts. Is that correct Inspector?"

Susana and Cornelia gave each other sideways glances.

Cornelia spoke first, "Certainly Inspector, we quite understand. My sister and I were here until about one thirty when we walked to the Tarts and Buns for lunch."

Susana, taking up the thread of the story with feeling continued, "And after lunch we stopped at Madame Sonia's to look at the latest winter fashions. That woman is so talented! Didn't we have fun

Cornelia?"

Sergeant Rogers, seeing that the Inspector was somewhat confused, explained, "Madame Sonia owns a women's clothing store in the village."

The inspector smiled and nodded trying to look interested. "Could I impose upon you to give us a time-line? It doesn't have to be exactly precise. An approximation will do."

Cornelia beat her sister to the punch. "Let's see, we must have gotten to the Tarts and Buns a little before two o'clock?" she looked at Susana not for confirmation but out of habit. "We met friends there and you know how it is when women get together." When she didn't receive any acknowledgement from either of the police officers she laughed nervously and continued, "Well we must have left the tea shop at oh, I'd say around, three thirty. I'm only just guessing, we weren't on a rigid schedule. And from there we went to Madame Sonia's." Again she looked at Susana. "I don't know how long we were there but I know that when we left it was getting dark."

"It was definitely around tea time," explained Susana. "I remember saying to Cornelia that we needed to get home in time for tea. But of course when we got home what with everything that happened we never even got our tea! Can you imagine?" and with a dignified nod of her head, folded her hands on her lap, and looked at the officers with a smile of satisfaction as if she had explained everything succinctly.

The inspector and his sergeant both looked up with raised brows. The Inspector had gone back to pondering about early retirement and the sergeant was busy taking down notes. Inspector Bunson had no wish to undermine Susana's somewhat sketchy account and quite possibly alienating a valuable if unwitting source of information.

But before he could ask her to elucidate, Jack, who was semi-conscious on an armchair but still holding on to his drink, opened one eye, looked at Susana with admiration and said, "Susana, you have the genius of Shakespeare!"

"Yes...er...Mrs. Leslie I believe you said that something had occurred which interrupted your tea?" prompted the Inspector.

"Oh yes, Inspector. Now let me see," Susana raised her finger to her chin and gazed up at the ceiling for inspiration, "As we've already said, Cornelia and I walked home from lunch and shopping." Looking pointedly at her sister she continue, "The health nut here always insists on walking. When we arrived home. Pinkey was all in a dither because her aunt was locked up so of course she hadn't time to finish the tea preparations which meant that we never did have our tea. Such a shame - don't you agree?"

Officer Rogers, seeing that the inspector began to unconsciously scrunch his hat, quickly changed tactics and addressing Susana said, "Very frustrating not having tea, isn't it?"

Turning to Cornelia he pleaded, "Perhaps if you could begin at the stage where you left Madame Sonia's?"

Cornelia's expressive face summed up the situation and with her intelligent eyes focused on Sergeant Rogers, said, "Yes, of course, I see exactly what you mean. After Madame Sonia's Susana and I decided that since it was getting dark, we'd walk round by Hunter's Bosk that is a twenty-minute walk - easily the quickest route back home. I'm sorry I can't give you the exact time we set off but if we got to the shop at around half past three – one does loose track of time when clothes shopping - it must have been somewhere around half past five when we left. When we were on the path that runs along the woods, we noticed a curious figure bolting from the woods and coming in our direction. When it got closer, we were surprised to see that it was Martha..."

Susana broke in, "That's right, it was most extraordinary how she didn't even answer us when we called out to her. In fact now that I look back on it I don't think she even saw us! She just zoomed past us with a queer look on her face as if she'd just seen a ghost. Why she almost ran us over! Didn't she Cornelia?"

Cornelia resumed the story, "We continued along the path home and it was obvious that Martha was heading in the same direction. When we arrived, Pinkey informed us that Martha had stormed into the house, and after making sure that all the doors and windows were locked, proceeded to lock herself up in her room. We were finally able to open the door with a duplicate key and calm her down with some sherry."

"It's kind of alarming to think that Martha could get any more peculiar," the Sergeant wondered out loud.

Susana jumped up from her chair and wringing her hands cried, "Oh Cornelia she's probably drowned in the bathtub! Do you think we're going to wind up in the 'big house'?" And with that she opened the door and ran down the hall towards the back of the house and Martha's room.

Sergeant Rogers was immediately behind her with the others close on his heels. When they reached

Martha's door it was once again locked and there was no answer to their pleas to allow them entry. The group remained expectantly huddled by the door until the sergeant asked Cornelia for the duplicate key. When they finally gained access they found Martha sprawled out on the bed clutching a bottle of bourbon.

"No wonder she's been so quiet. She's out cold!" concluded Sergeant Rogers.

"Well really, you didn't have to give her the '*Wild Turkey*'! And to think that I limit myself to one drink before bed," remarked Jack sadly appraising Martha's black out.

"Ooo sorry, Mr. Jack." Everyone turned around to look at a round-eyed Pinkey who was standing just outside the door. "But that's not the bottle I gave Auntie. When Mrs. C. said to give her a glass of sherry I brought the bottle knowing that she'd need more than just one itty-bitty glass. Oh there's the bottle on the floor!"

"Oh no, not the '*Jerez*' sherry. Pinkey, please tell me you didn't give her the bottle of Jerez," appealed Jack.

Pinkey, now looking more distressed than when her aunt was in the midst of her peculiar dramatics, said, "Is that an expensive bottle? Gee, I just grabbed the first bottle that said 'sherry' on the label like Mrs. C. told me. You have ever so many bottles in your bar Mr. Jack! A person can't be reading every one of 'em!"

Jack, with his charming smile replied, "Don't mind me Pinkey, you're entirely correct. I must do something about all that liquor in the bar. It's disgraceful. In fact, I think I'll start immediately."

Inspector Bunson, having picked up Martha's key from the floor took both keys and escorting everyone out of the room said, "We're not going to get anything out of her tonight but we are going to need to speak with her in the morning. Until then, if you don't mind, I'm going to place a constable outside her door."

The Scotland Yard detectives bid goodnight to the sisters and followed Jack to the door. Standing on the parquet floor of the entry hall. Sergeant Rogers pointed to the Persian rug and with admiration said, "Exquisite rug this. The brick red coloring with the central medallion and the flowering tendrils – I'll bet it's a Kashan. Beautiful pattern."

Jack, taken aback by the Sergeant's knowledge of Persian rugs, replied, "Yes, it's been in the family for eons. I really don't know much about it except that it's old and Persian, and that name sounds familiar. The girls would know more if you're really interested."

"Yes...thanks...definitely will ask," replied Rogers bending down to study a corner of the carpet.

Inspector Bunson stared at Rogers in bewilderment. Alarmed that the Sergeant was at risk of shaming the force with his aesthetic sensibilities, he murmured, "Sergeant, I think we'd better let Mr. Leslie go to bed. We'll be back tomorrow to interview Martha."

Sergeant Rogers looked up chagrined. "Oh, I'm sorry, sir. I was just noticing that there's a fresh spot of mud on the corner of the rug."

The inspector walked over to take a closer look. "You're right. It is fresh and definitely an imprint of a heel."

"Well that's country living for you. But don't let the girls know–they'll be mortified. Unfortunate how difficult it is to find good help these days," said

Jack with a bemused look.

Inspector Bunson self-consciously looked down at his shoes to see if he had any earth stuck to the soles. Then he walked out into the chill of an autumn night.

When the officers had gotten back in the car, the inspector looked at his sergeant, "Rogers, you completely astound me. Wherever did you learn about Persian carpets?"

"Rugs Inspector? Oh, that was just a lead up to the mud on the rug. Good pick up that, don't you think? I put some in my pocket for testing," replied the Rogers.

"Nice job. We'll need to verify his story of course. But like Mr. Leslie said, it's not unusual to track mud around when you live in the country." He continued to stare in puzzlement at his sergeant.

With the day's latest developments fresh in their minds, the police officers headed back to the station a little before midnight. Rogers, cognizant of the work ahead of them, wasted no time and ordered coffee and sandwiches.

Both men sat at their desks looking over the notes on the case. The Inspector reviewing hard copies while Rogers worked on his computer.

Taking a sip from his steaming mug, Inspector Bunson let out a swear and set down the mug with a thud that drenched the papers which he had been studying.

"How in the dickens do they get this coffee to stay at boiling point?" he asked when he was able to speak. Then looking at the mess on his desk, "You're going to have to print a new set of notes, these are ruined."

"No worries – jeez, all that liquid came out of

one mug? Have you ever noticed how when something spills it looks as if it had filled twice the container it came from? I guess that's one of life's little mysteries."

"Speaking of mysteries, that manor is a looney bin. And I don't just mean the help. Those siblings, do they always act that way or is it just for my benefit?"

Sergeant Rogers smiled, "The Leslie's? That family is famous for being eccentric. Every Leslie since the year one has had that trait. But they're all as smart as a whip, every single one of them." Rogers looked at his superior who had his brows puckered, "I know what you're thinking. It's kind of funny how in the village of Epping we have two polar opposite families each with quirky family traits that have been passed down through generations. The locals tend to think the Jenkins' as harebrained dullards – except for Pinkey – while the
Leslies are just campy and flaky with high IQ's. They've always been good to the Village too. Never have to ask a Leslie twice when it comes to contributions or donations."

A knock at the door, brought a constable with a note which he handed to Rogers. Reading the note, Sergeant Rogers said, "It seems that Moe Stone called earlier this evening. He was walking through Hunter's Bosk on his way home from the pub at about nine o'clock at night when he heard a moan. Thought it was kids and took no notice."

Inspector Bunson interrupted, "Don't tell me. The *village telegraph* has been efficiently spreading the latest news. Go have one of the constables call the pub owner to verify Moe Stone's alibi."

The information obtained from Bert Colby of

the Raven's Roost alluded to several of the persons in question being at the pub between the hours of four in the afternoon and closing at ten o'clock. There was a darts tournament in progress that night so there was plenty of movement with a lively crowd. He couldn't be sure as to the exact times people came in but he thought that Moe might have left earlier than most.

Chapter 19

As if the previous day and evening hadn't had enough complications, the early morning continued to bring new developments. The Scotland Yard detectives were informed that Betty Smith's prognosis had turned for the worse.

The officers had just gotten off the phone with the hospital when Jim McCarthy was shown into their office.

"Thanks for your time. I gather it's been a long night," he said pulling a chair from a corner. "I've already been to the site. Constable Jenkins is guarding the area as if his life depended on it. I made his day by snapping his picture."

Sergeant Rogers, who had been concentrating on his computer screen, snorted and said, "Yeah, he's been involved in more police activity in the past few days than he has since he enrolled in the force. He's having a field day." Then turning serious, he continued, "How is it that you were present at the dinner party on the night of Julia Peters' death?"

"That's an easy one. I had a formal invitation from the Leslies. And interestingly, Julia also called me to make sure that I was invited because as she put it, 'It would make good copy.' I'm a newspaperman and I never turn down a lead. Besides which Julia was involved in every detail in the life of this village and

I've learned, as have most people in this village, that Julia was not above getting her own way in anything she put her mind to. I'm hoping for a lead to that one individual who did us all a favor."

"Wow, talk about freaky. Little did she know that she was going to be the front page story for days," mused Sergeant Rogers.

"And in more than one paper! They're picking up my stories all across England! I don't want to sound gruesome but I'm reveling in all this as much if not more than our good constable! Which brings me to why I came to the station today."

Ignoring this last bit, the inspector asked, "Were you always associated with journalism? I believe you told our staff that you worked at a small trade paper in London as a copy editor before you moved to Epping."

"That's right. Ran it with my wife for twelve years. Then after she died, I decided to chuck it all and move to the country. Something I always wanted to do."

"What made you decide on Epping? There's thousands of small villages throughout England," asked the inspector with interest.

The editor looked at both men before speaking. With a slight grimace he replied, "I was distraught after my wife died from ovarian cancer so I sought medical help. My internist referred me to a shrink who diagnosed me as clinically depressed and put me on medication, which seemed to help. After a few weeks, I decided to sell our house and get out of London. I wanted a complete change of scenery and I worked with house agents looking for a place in the country or seaside. I settled on Epping. The fact that the village didn't have a newspaper was the clincher."

"Hmm," nodded Inspector Bunson reflecting that he wouldn't mind retiring to a quiet spot in the country with nothing to do but fish all day. "It *is* beautiful country out here. I suppose you enjoyed getting away from all the noise and pollution of a big city. Do you fish by any chance?"

The editor looked amused. "No Inspector, I don't fish. I'm too much of an "A" type personality to sit around waiting for something to happen. As you said, we don't have noise or pollution to worry about in the country. And after living in an overpopulated city that can be very enticing. But in my case, after a while, the charm and allure of the countryside began to get a bit stagnating. Except for the past few days life in Epping is more or less the same everyday."

"That's for sure," murmured Rogers under his breath.

Jim McCarthy gave a shadow of a grin. "The fascinating thing about living in a village is its citizens and their interaction with one another. Unless you've lived it, it's difficult to understand the dynamics that play into village life. It's been a real eye opener to a city dweller who's used to being invisible and just another body in the masses going to and from wherever." He continued animatedly, "This place gave me a new insight into human behavior."

The chief Inspector swallowed a yawn and going over to the coat rack said, "Yes, I'm beginning to see that you've provided the village and town a valuable service." Unable to stifle another yawn, he continued, "Rogers, I'm going to go home and get some sleep. You can fill in Mr. McCarthy with the latest developments."

Chapter 21

The necessity of having a police constable on guard inside the house only increased Susana's sleeplessness. She got up from bed at an early hour and headed downstairs. Once in the back hall she purposely averted her eyes from the direction of Martha's room and headed towards the kitchen. In an effort to calm her nerves she began preparations for a lavish breakfast. She began by making herself a large cup of cappuccino with extra cream and a good sprinkling of extra-fine cocoa powder. Next, she went to the four bookcases which stood at one end of a long, marble baking counter and pulled out the binder labeled 'Breakfast'. Susana was meticulous in the organization of her recipes and only the best-loved recipes found their way into the binders. She sat at the desk that occupied a niche in between the bookcases and began rifling through the pages. After just a few minutes, she walked over to the professional size refrigerator/freezer scanning its cavernous space to make sure that she had all the ingredients she'd need. She would start out with scrambled eggs with smoked salmon and chives and of course some bacon rashers fried to just the right crispiness. This would be accompanied by homemade bread, baked yesterday morning, sliced and fried in the bacon fat. Susana, who was not overly fond of fresh fruit, compensated by taking out a jar of marmalade. After mulling between flaky, buttery croissants and something a little sweeter, she settled on the side of her sweet tooth.

Susana was not the only person at the manor who had spent the night tossing and turning. Her sister Cornelia had had an equally sleepless night and in the early dawn as she finally drifted in and out of sleep, the light in a chink of the curtains awakened her enough to sharpen her hearing. She lay listening to muffled noises. At first, Cornelia feared that Martha had somehow escaped the Constable on duty and gotten out of her room. She quickly put on her robe and slippers and in the silvery light of dawn made her way down the stairs anxiously thinking up ways in which to coerce Martha back to bed.

Once in the back hall, Cornelia came upon an agitated Constable Jenkins pulling on the doorknob of Martha's door while hissing in a stage whisper for Martha to 'Stop yur caterwaulin'!' From behind the door Martha could be heard howling to be let out.

The cacophony coming from both sides of the door was more than Cornelia's splitting head could stand. With remarkable self control, Cornelia asked, "I'm sorry to interrupt you Constable Jenkins but how long has Martha been awake?"

Making a hasty about face, Jenkins replied, "Mornin' M'am. She just awoke not two minutes ago. I s'ppose all that rattlin' in the kitchen woke her." To Cornelia's amusement, he raised his head and took a whiff as the enticing aroma of food reached his nostrils.

"You don't look like you've had any sleep, Constable. Why don't you just sit down and in a few minutes, after I speak with Martha, I'll get you some breakfast," replied Cornelia trying to guide Jenkins to a chair.

"Well, I s'ppose a little food might do me good. I ain't 'ad a wink of sleep. What with the lady found in 'unter's Bosk last night and then no sooner I get 'ome to bed than I get called back on duty on account of old Dibbs needs 'is rest and I 'ave to take over baby sittin ' Miss 'issyfit 'ere," replied Jenkins expansively.

"Well now if you'll just give me the key, I'll go in and calm Martha down. She might want a bit of breakfast," answered Cornelia with an air of innocence.

The constable scrunched his face in an effort to think out this predicament. With an uncertain tone he replied, "I don't knows if I'm s'pposed to let anyone in M'am."

Cornelia was saved from using any further psychological warfare by the persistent appetizing aromas emitting from the vicinity of the kitchen.

"Well I s'ppose I could do with just a bite or two," replied the constable taking out the key from his pocket and giving it to Cornelia.

"That's fine. You just go on over to the kitchen and Mrs. S. will be more than happy to give you breakfast."

Cornelia knocked on Martha's door and in her most soothing voice said, "Martha, it's Mrs. C. I'm coming in." As Cornelia stepped into the room she somehow willed herself to overcome the urge to burst out laughing.

In front of her, Martha stood in what Cornelia assumed was a representation of a karate pose. One bony leg in front of the other in a squatting stance, with her arms raised and bent at the elbows and her hands stretched out with fingers pointing up at the ceiling. If possible, Martha's red hair was more out of control than usual and her light red eyebrows and lashes blended in with her freckles canceling out the desired intimidating expression.

Adding to the ridiculous, Martha cautioned, "I'm an expert Ninja warrior so don't try anythin' funny! And you can tell that snivelin' Billy that I'm gonna have fun showin' 'im some of my moves!"

"Come off it Martha, you don't really think that I'm going to hurt you. And Billy was just doing his job. Besides, you were in such a state yesterday that it was for your own good that we locked the door. What are you so afraid of?"

Martha walked backwards towards the bed keeping her wild eyes glued on Cornelia. Then sitting up against the pillows, knees up against her chest, with the bedclothes covering everything except her eyes, she gave a shudder and murmured, "Nothin', do you 'ear, nothin'! Now leave me alone! I ain't seen nothin'!" and she began a rhythmic swaying forwards and backwards.

Cornelia went up to the bed and sat down. "Martha you know you're safe here. We would never let anyone hurt you. If you saw something that frightened you yesterday, please tell me. You're going to have a nervous breakdown if you continue like this."

The door opened and in walked a flustered Susana her cheeks and red apron covered in flour.

"Good morning Martha! So nice to see that you're awake. You must have a blinding headache, shall I get you some aspirin?"

Pulling down the covers to show a defiant

curled lip, Martha replied, "An "eadache? Now why should I 'ave an 'eadache?" Suddenly she gasped and her already pale face drained of what little color it had. She pulled at the covers and in a frightened whisper said, "'O said anythin' about me 'ead! No one's coshin' me 'ead again! See? I ain't gonna be murdered like that lady in 'unter's Bosk!"

Susana's hand went to her mouth trying to stifle a scream. "Cornelia, what does she mean? What lady – do you think she means Betty?" Not waiting to hear Cornelia's response, she turned to Martha and with more confidence than she felt, said, "Oh, Martha dear, everything's going to be fine. You just had a little too much to drink last night. You just lay back and I'll bring you some breakfast. Your cousin Billy is on his third helping! He does have a big appetite doesn't he?"

Martha's silent appraisal of the two women was a combination of panic and scorn. Her eyelids flickered and Cornelia quickly realized that Martha's terror was succumbing to exhaustion.

"Good idea, Susana. Martha, you can do with some food. No one will be allowed to get into your room because I have the only key and I'm not letting it out of my sight." Closing the door, she turned to Susana and said, "Martha saw something in Hunter's Bosk yesterday. That's why she stampeded back here. We have to find out what she saw."

When the two sisters got to the kitchen they found Pinkey cheerfully serving up breakfast to a happy horde of people. While the two women were with Martha, Jack had joined Billy at the table followed by both Inspector Bunson and Sergeant Rogers. The table was sagging under the platters of food and every one of the men had a plate piled high with bacon, eggs, tomatoes, fried bread and cinnamon buns. Not to mention mugs of steaming coffee and tea.

"Mrs. S., this is the best food I've eaten in a long time. I don't know if I can go back to the Java Bar after this meal!" exclaimed Rogers.

Inspector Bunson chimed in, "Thank you for your hospitality. Nothing's better than a really good English breakfast."

"Really? You don't know how pleased that makes me – or do you?"

Cornelia turned to the police officers. "Martha was quite agitated again this morning so I thought it a good idea to go in and calm her down. After all, she's been with us for years and I would hope she trusts us."

"Strewth, she were yellin' a 'oly terror. 'ow you both came out in one piece I'll never know." snorted Constable Jenkins his mouth full of cinnamon buns.

Using a napkin to hide a smile, Jack replied, "You haven't lived with my sisters. When it's a question of survival of the fittest, I'll put my money on the girls any day."

Martha's respite didn't last very long. Before the two sisters had finished making up her breakfast tray, she could be heard pounding on the door. The two officers immediately got up and headed for the door with Cornelia running after them.

"Let me calm her down before you go in. I know we're all used to Martha's hysterics but this time she's definitely terrified of something or someone and I don't want to think what she'd do if you go in without my warning her," said Cornelia hastily getting in front of the officers.

After several knocks without response, they opened the door and found Martha under the covers. With one swift movement she suddenly sat up holding the covers to her face and only revealing one red eye that stared fearfully around the room. From under the covers could be heard Martha's voice saying, "I weren't asleep so don't try nothin'! No one's gonna murder me in my own bed!"

Cornelia took a deep breath and asked, " Did you have anything to drink or eat this morning?"

"Course not, I ain't gonna touch no food nor drink that I ain't prepared myself! You think I'm crazy or somethin'?" replied Martha with feeling.

Cornelia bit her tongue before she told Martha what she really thought and then said, "Really, why would we try to poison you? Stop being so silly! Mike Rogers is here with Inspector Bunson and they'd like to speak with you. And before you go having hysterics, I'll stay with you so you don't have to be afraid. In any case, they're police officers and they're here to protect you," and with that she motioned to the officers to come in.

Keeping on the safe side, Inspector Bunson nudged Rogers in front of him.

Martha had decided to hide under the covers and play dead. When this contrivance failed to hoodwink the officers, she bolted to a sitting position and between shrieks and moans, expressed her certainty that she was going to be the 'maniac killer's' next victim. With remarkable restraint and after several words of reassurance that they would make sure of her safety, the officers managed to extract a somewhat coherent description of the events of the previous day.

Chapter 22

Having spent a laborious morning at the manor, the bedraggled and exhausted Scotland Yard detectives made their escape into a gray and sodden countryside. Martha, who insisted that she would not leave her room until the 'psycho-killer' was apprehended, was left in Pinkey's capable hands and the Leslie sisters were finally able to settle down to their own breakfast.

"I still can't believe how Martha does it. You'd think with all that she had to drink she'd be comatose. Wouldn't you?" wondered Susana as she served herself a third helping of bacon.

Cornelia, who was pushing the food around her plate, sipped her coffee and replied, "I'm still trying to filter through Martha's story."

Susana shuddered and dropped her fork, "Oooh, let's not talk about that, it's too awful to contemplate. A killer right here in Hunter's Bosk! Aren't you terrified?"

Mother Nature answered with a terrific bolt of lightning followed by a resounding crack and the room was plunged into sudden darkness.

With speed that matched the offending lightning, Susana was in the hallway holding her apron to her mouth in the hope that it would stifle any screams. She was grabbed by her brother who had been on his way to check the fuse box in the basement and was efficiently guided back to the kitchen with reassurances that the power outage was due to weather and not a homicidal maniac.

With the electricity restored so was Susana's self-confidence. Once again seated at the kitchen table with a plate of cinnamon buns in front of her, she gave an artificial laugh and said, "Doesn't lightning always seem a little scarier in the country?"

"Susana, you seem to forget that we were on the lane that goes past Hunter's Bosk at the same time that Martha says she past Betty's body. Which can only mean that we were only a few hundred feet from not only her but possibly her attacker."

"Must you be so gruesome?" gasped Susana with a look of horror. Using a piece of fried bread to push eggs onto her fork, she took a bite and with a sigh added, "If there's a killer loose in Epping then Mikey Rogers and that nice old Inspector will just have to try harder to catch him! I mean I'm always happy to have people enjoy my cooking but if there really *is* a killer walking about the village what is the entire police force doing eating breakfast in our kitchen?"

"Hmm, that's exactly what I was thinking," expressed Cornelia, once again marveling at how her sister could be both vague and astute all in the same breath. "I'm beginning to think that Rogers and Bunson could use a little help. How do you feel about conducting our own investigation?"

Susana dropped her fork and stared at her sister in amazement. "Oh really Cornelia, I know we loved Nancy Drew and we did have our own Nancy Drew club as youngsters but don't you think that's taking things too far?"

Cornelia flashed stubbornly and replied, "No, I don't. I'm quite serious. Martha has implicated both of us with the story she gave the police! So who better to do some behind the scenes snooping than us?"

"Do you really mean that nice Inspector suspects *us*?" asked Susana in horror.

"Heavens to Murgatroyd, of course they can! In fact we, along with Jack are probably at the top of their list of suspects. Once again, your selective memory has forgotten that Julia died in our home after ingesting poison in food cooked in our kitchen." Cornelia kindly left out the fact that Susana was instrumental in the preparation of the meal. "And, we just happened to be in the area where Betty's body was found. Not to mention that Jack was - to put it mildly - friendly with Betty and is basically without an alibi for a good part of the late afternoon and evening on the night she was found."

Susana put her napkin to her mouth and gave a little squeak. "Oh my gosh, we could be arrested at any minute!" Then wringing her hands added, "Should we go to the police station and beg for mercy?"

"No, it's not as bad as all that – yet. I think we'll start our snooping by paying the vicar a visit. After all, we haven't been to the vicarage in a few days and we can bring him some of your cinnamon buns." She looked around for the pan but saw an empty platter with a few crumbs.

Susana, following her sister's line of vision, responded, "I'll make an apple pie for Thomas. He's always loved my pies and it won't take me long at all." She frowned and continued, "You're not thinking of walking in this weather are you?"

By the time they arrived at the vicarage, the black clouds had begun to disperse and a disheartened sun was trying its best to peek through. However with capricious humor, Mother Nature added a frigid chill that foretold the arrival of a frost.

The sisters noticed that the vicar's car was not inside the barn. "We might as well go and knock on the door and give Mrs. Hardy the pie. Vicar is probably out doing his parish rounds. We can leave the pie and he can have it with his tea, okay?" volunteered Susana.

Cornelia decided that the loquacious housekeeper might be even more chatty without the presence of her employer and readily agreed to seek out Mrs. Hardy.

Sure enough, the door was opened almost immediately by a red faced Mrs. Hardy who was holding a dust mop in her large, pudgy hands. Her expression as she opened the door was that of someone who had been rudely interrupted at her work. However upon seeing the Leslie sisters the expression changed to a beaming smile and with her Scotch burr said, "Why it's the Mrs. Leslies! A fine mornin' to you. Goodness, the vicar never said anything about expecting you ladies to come a'callin' today. But here now, I see you've vera kindly brought him a beauty of a pie! Poor dear, he's been worried sick with all that's been happenin'. I have the kettle going, and in two shakes of a lamb's tail we can have a nice chat." She waived them in and still carrying the mop quickly walked towards the hall that lead to the only warm room in the house. Mrs. Hardy pushed two chairs out from the highly polished kitchen table and motioned the sisters to sit down. The kettle at the old-fashioned Aga stove was singing in no time and Mrs. Hardy deftly poured out strong black tea along with a tin of shortbread that she placed in front of the two women.

"Oooo, *'Petticoat Tails'*! I can't resist shortbread. I was hoping you'd have some on hand! Aren't they delicious?" exclaimed Susana as she reached inside the tin.

Mrs. Hardy gave a throaty chortle, "Hm, the vicar always enjoys his shortbread. O'course now he can have as much as he pleases. Not like as when the old dragon was around – and no good saying as not on account she's passed!" she flashed, compressing her lips into a thin line.

"Well that just goes to show you, I always thought it was my cooking that he enjoyed so much. But come to think of it, he always did eat with more gusto when Julia wasn't around. That should teach me a lesson not to be so proud. I guess his sister was starving him. Oh dear, did I just say that?" remarked Susana with alarm.

In any other situation, Cornelia would have winced at Susana's frankness. But now she sat back enjoying the spontaneous commentary.

As if tasting bitter lemons, Mrs. Hardy pursed her lips, "That woman bullied the poor soul something fierce! O' course, she'd never be caught dead sayin' anythin' to him in public. She'd just look at him with a sad, martyred look on her face and he'd immediately stop eatin' or speakin' or lookin'. I tell you it was enough to make a person sick!" she slammed her cup down making Susana jump. "Sorry Mrs. S., I don't mean to talk ill of the dead but what's right is right and no one can say different. That woman enjoyed keepin' her brother tethered to her apron strings. He's a saint, that's what he is to have put up with that harridan for so long. Many's the time when he'd be in his solarium quietly tendin' his flowers or readin' until she found him and then with snide remarks she'd make him feel guilty for not being in that frozen tundra of a study. So selfish and self-important she was. She could go for weekends alone to London but her brother couldn't do anythin' without her being right there beside him. Why the only time he'd be allowed to go anywhere alone was when she was busy presidin' over one of her committees – the malevolent old prune."

Susana shook her head in agreement dipping her hand into the shortbread tin, "Dear me, she was rather bossy wasn't she? To tell you the truth I was a little afraid of her – nil nisi bonum – she had a way of making me feel like an idiot." Warming to her subject she continued, "I mean she never actually said anything it's just the way she'd look at me – remember the flower committee Cornelia? She used her position as president to re-arrange every vase in the church and no one had the nerve to tell her that her arrangements were hideous, did they?" Susana looked at Mrs. Hardy for emphasis. Remember how she liked to put the vegetables in with the flowers and one time at the Harvest Service a couple of the vases waited until the vicar was starting his sermon to topple over! You could feel the tension in the air with some of the women giggling and others furious that their prized vegetables and flowers were decorating the floor!" sputtered Susana bent over in laughter. Regaining her composure she continued, "Julia just sat there with her eyes closed acting as if she was above any earthly disruption. Really her nerve was *beyond* beyond. Wasn't it Cornelia? Cornelia, are you paying attention?"

"Hmm? Oh, yes, it was funny. Mrs. Hardy, was Julia in the habit of going up to London on a regular basis?" asked Cornelia.

"If you call once a month regular," observed the housekeeper with feeling. "She'd just tell her brother at breakfast on Friday that she'd be goin' to visit friends in London after breakfast – never thought of invitin' him to go along. No, she was a selfish, bitter old nag. And I'm not sorry to say it!"

Cornelia wasn't paying attention. She was still pondering Julia's frequent trips to London. Aware of Mrs. Hardy's theatrical pause awaiting her audience's appreciation, she made the required astonished noises and then asked the housekeeper how long Julia stayed away.

"Always back for Sunday church. My goodness, she was the one to put on airs about piety and attendin' church services. But goodness knows, she wasn't foolin' me! But the poor vicar, now that's a different story, never saw past his nose when it came to his sister. No sir, he's just too good for his own good," remarked Mrs. Harding frowning.

Suddenly the front door was heard opening and two male voices could be heard laughing in the entry.

Finishing the last shortbread in the tin, Susana wiped the crumbs off her dress and the sisters thanked Mrs. Hardy for her kindness.

"Now don't you go thankin' me for anythin'! I'm sure I've enjoyed this chat more than you have," replied Mrs. Hardy.

Just as the sisters were heading to the kitchen door, they nearly bumped into the vicar who had come to ask Mrs. Hardy for some refreshments in the vicarage solarium.

"Well this is a pleasure!" said the vicar embracing both women. "Sam Taylor is here and we're going to go over some landscaping plans for the back garden. I've been hoping to put in a lily pond there for years! Please join us, I can use some feminine suggestions," he continued excitedly.

Greeting the handsome farmer the sisters' demeanor quickly changed. Susana, who was always flustered in his presence, kept nervously fussing with her hair until the pins holding her sophisticated French bun began to slowly fall out keeping her bending down to pick them up only to refasten them crookedly into her hair.

"Isn't this nice. So much nicer than when we last met – but of course that was horrible…er…what I mean to say is what happened that night was horrible. Oh, the whole thing has me so flustered I don't know what I'm saying – do I?" she managed to mumble with her mouth full of bobby pins.

The Leslies and Sam Taylor followed the vicar from the warm and cozy kitchen through damp corridors to the solarium. It was a favorite joke with the vicar that he had to put on an extra sweater before going into this room and the wood stove was kept continually running. However due to the room's three sided glass walls and high glass ceiling, only the area within ten feet of the stove was actually comfortably warm. Everyone who entered the room was amazed at the exotic plants and other fauna that happily thrived in the inclement environment. It was local gossip that maintained that this was the result of Providence's favor towards the vicar.

"This room is so inspiring – and the fragrance!

Why I don't think our sunroom has this many orchids or even any orchids. Do we Cornelia?" observed Susana.

"The flowers you're able to grow here are absolutely magnificent," remarked Cornelia walking over to a particularly lovely peony. "Oh, this is the fragrance that's been permeating the room! This must be a late blooming peony!"

The vicar joined her and with pride showing all over his face, he beamed, "That's right. One of my prize peonies. It's a Karl Rosenfeld, very showy don't you think? Of course I have the peony garden at the side garden but they're such a beautiful flowers I enjoy having them inside."

Mrs. Hardy walked in carrying a tray with glasses and a decanter of sherry. "Thank you Mrs. Hardy. Now if I can serve everyone a glass of sherry? I do enjoy a glass before lunch."

Cornelia and Susana looked up in alarm, "Oh, but we couldn't possibly stay for lunch, vicar. I made my special apple pie for your tea and we decided to personally deliver it but of course you weren't here when we arrived so Mrs. Hardy was kind enough to invite us for elevenses. I practically devoured the entire tin of her shortbread and I couldn't possibly eat another morsel! Could I?" replied Susana looking at her sister.

"And I just dropped by to help you with the configuration of the pond and to bring you some compost for your marrows. I don't mind saying that I'd enjoy staying for one of Mrs. Hardy's delicious meals but I've got a meeting in town that I can't miss," added Sam.

"Well then how about some sherry and a walk around the garden. I'll tell you about my plans for a lily pond and you can give me your suggestions," responded the vicar handing out the sherry.

Everyone sat around the inviting wood stove, and after handing each of his guests a glass of sherry, the vicar poured one for himself and leaned back in his chair. It was obvious to all that he was happy in this room.

Cornelia could not stop thinking about a remark of Mrs. Hardy's and decided that if she didn't speak up now, she'd never have the nerve again. Bracing herself with a large sip of sherry she said, "It's so pleasant and cozy sitting here surrounded by all this natural beauty. Julia must have loved this room."

The vicar suddenly looked very tired and then realizing that it had gotten very quiet and three pairs of eyes were staring at him, he responded, "I used to hope that she'd grow to enjoy it as much as I did." Then his voice trailed off and with an embarrassed shrug he continued, "She never cared for anything which required continuous attention."

Susana had initially been frozen in place at the uncharacteristic solecism made by her sister but receiving a sisterly look from Cornelia she immediately caught on and with remarkable presence of mind said, "Oh I understand completely, I myself am very happy to sit in our sunroom at home but if forced to choose, I would definitely prefer to spend the day shopping in town followed by an evening of taste testing at various restaurants."

It was now Cornelia's turn to try and hide the look of disbelief on her face. The idea that comfy Susana was or ever had been a party girl was ludicrous in the least. The mental picture of Susana partying it up brought a twitch to Cornelia's lips.

The vicar returned to his former self, and smiling said, "You're absolutely right, Susana! Julia loved going up to London. She'd go and spend long weekends with friends there." As if in explanation he added, "My sister was a great admirer of art and theatre."

Cornelia uttered what had been on everyone's mind, "And did you ever accompany her vicar?"

"No-o-o, she preferred going by herself. I understood. She had her own friends and I'd be in the way – a little brother again, if you know what I mean."

The three guests, already feeling more than a little uncomfortable, favored the vicar's attempt at lighthearted humor with smiles.

"Well if you ask me, Julia was fortunate in having friends with whom she could stay. These days it costs an arm and a leg to just go out for a nice dinner in London much less staying at a first rate hotel. Such a shame, isn't it?" observed Susana expansively while avoiding looking at her sister.

The vicar smiled, and slowly reaching for the sherry decanter began to refill everyone's glass. "My sister was the beneficiary of a trust left by an aunt of ours. She had independent means and was fairly rich even by today's standards." The sisters exchanged knowing glances.

Getting up rather unsteadily, the vicar continued, "If everyone is ready, I'd be honored to show you round the gardens."

"Lovely! It's just about the time when your marrows are growing to the size of a house! Are we going to get to see them?" asked Cornelia.

The vicar beamed with pleasure and with an embarrassed chuckle answered, "You know I'm sinfully proud of my marrows. I start looking through the seed catalogues immediately after the season is over and all through winter I research the best method for growing them into giants."

"And well you should be! Taking first prize for the past five years at the county fair isn't easy! In fact, I've been meaning to tell you that if your marrows get any bigger we're going to have to use the hay wagons to transport them to the fair!" jested the farmer.

Everyone laughed and followed the justifiably proud vicar out to the expansive kitchen garden which lay at one side of the vicarage and which was walled in by a beautiful honey brick wall. The garden was formally partitioned with squares edged in miniature boxwood and devoted to all the commonly used herbs and some not so common varieties such as lemon thyme, lovage, columbine, lemon balm, borage and feverfew. The vegetables also were planted in block plantings with English runner beans growing up a trellis of string tied to poles. There were peas, potatoes, cabbage, and cucumbers planted alongside lettuces, onions and leeks. There were edible flowers such as nasturtiums and violas bordered by marigolds that the vicar was sure warded off pests. The squares were surrounded by walkways of brick in between which grew tiny tufts of moss and along the brick wall were planted pleached pear and peach trees.

Although Susana was not a lover of the outdoors as were her host and fellow guests, she found it difficult to resist the heady culinary scents and sights which enveloped her as she walked along the path. At every turn of her head she was met with the provender of her art in a state of freshness and perfection. Even the leaves that swirled around her feet could not dampen her enthusiasm. And it was with many oohs and aahs that she joined in the compliments given to the vicar. "Really vicar, it takes my breath away whenever I visit your kitchen garden. I don't believe there's another as lovely in all of Epping. One never knows where to look. It's like a candy store for chefs! Isn't it?" exclaimed Susana.

"Yes, you put us to shame, vicar!" added Cornelia laughing. "I know that Julia was very proud of the gardens here," she continued with false innocence.

The vicar slowly bent down and reached for a nonexistent weed, and briefly answered, "Julia took pride in the specimens she would take to decorate the church."

"And that's why she was voted president of the Garden Association because no one would dare oppose her. They knew they couldn't compete with even a blade of grass here! Could they?" remarked Susana guilelessly turning around to survey the bounty.

Sam Taylor pinched off a piece of lemon balm to put in his mouth. Purposely staring at the bees that continually hovered around that herb, Sam volunteered, "I remember as a boy having to drink an infusion of this whenever I'd have a tooth coming in."

"Julia was a very committed member of the community," uttered the vicar still avoiding looking at his guests. "She got great pleasure in presiding over committees. Well Cornelia, I think you wanted to see my marrows?" He asked taking her arm and leading the party to a door in the corner of the back wall.

The contrast between the two planting areas was unmistakable yet equally astounding. The previous had striking differences of shape, texture, color and scent, while the present vista was a green sea of large vines covering a large rectangular area. At intervals giant marrows lay in repose looking as if they were right out of the story, '*Jack and the Beanstalk*'. Acting like children at an egg hunt, Sam, Cornelia, and Susana each ran to oogle a different marrow marveling at their size and pointing out their individual features.

Sam Taylor was the most enthusiastic in his praise, "It takes quite a bit of time and patience to grow these and when they do grow to this size, more often than not they crack just when you're about to take 'em to the fair! I see some good specimens here Tom. This one here's got to be near one hundred pounds."

"I have a delicious soup recipe for marrows which I've been wanting to try this autumn! Haven't I Cornelia?" cried Susana excitedly as she walked over to inspect the super giant marrow. "Oh my heavens, how do you even pick that up? Actually I don't think I have a soup pot large enough to handle that size marrow, do I?" she said her eyes closed in an effort to think. Opening her eyes and with her hands on her hips and brows knitted she stared at the giant vegetable making a great effort to solve her dilemma. "Hmm, I bet six large soup pots would do the trick. Don't you?" she said looking out into the distance with visions of cold winter nights and dozens of hot bowls of creamy vegetable soup.

The vicar chuckled, "The Harvest Festival is right around the corner. I'm sure you'd have plenty of people eager to sample your culinary masterpieces if you're willing to go to the trouble. I'd be more than happy to supply the vegetables and help in any way."

Susana answered delightedly. "Oh of course,

how silly of me, the Harvest Festival! Julia always delegated me to the cleanup crew. It will be a welcome change to serve up some home cooking! And thank you very much Vicar I'd love to have you help. You can follow directions can't you?"

"Now Vicar, with Julia in the house I'm sure you didn't have to worry about cooking! At every town meeting she'd regale us about the delicious meals she prepared for you. I'm not fooling when I say she had our mouths watering every time!" declared Sam not without a little malice.

Knowing that Julia's stories of her culinary aptitude were just stories, Cornelia and Susana had the dignity to look uncomfortable and both began talking at once.

Susana looked at the vicar and said, "I think Julia only meant that she helped the housekeeper with the cooking. She didn't really do the cooking. Isn't that right Vicar?"

"Quite right Susana. I'm ashamed to say that Julia felt that cooking was beneath her. She'd give the housekeeper instructions on what she liked to eat and how she liked it prepared but she very rarely set foot in the kitchen. I wish I had known about those stories. This is the first I hear of them. I guess Julia felt she had to excel at everything."

A sudden lull in the conversation urged Sam to say in a jocular tone, "How 'bout taking us to see where you want that lily pond, vicar. It's getting late and I've still got a lunch meeting to attend."

This produced the desired effect and the vicar conveyed his guests with enthusiastic descriptions of his plans. After about thirty minutes of animated discussion, with each of the guests expressing their ideas of the design, the vicar was left with a jumble of notes that would take a miracle to decode.

    Saying their goodbyes, the sisters decided to walk around the house to their car affording them and especially Cornelia, a walk through the secluded 'Rose Room'.

Chapter 23

As they walked along the gravel path, admiring the roses bordered on four sides by huge boxwood giving the impression of a 'room' within the garden, Susana noticed someone waving to them from a small building with large windows that functioned as a potting shed for the vicar's garden.

"Look Cornelia, I think that's Mrs. Hardy waving to us. Do you think she could have another of her baked goods for us? All this walking and talking about food has made me ravenous. Aren't you hungry?" This was a rhetorical question because she was already half way to the shed and out of hearing range of her sister.

"Oh Mrs. S. what you must think of me wavin' my arms at you and Mrs. C.," apologized Mrs. Hardy. "It's just that before Miss Peters died I saw somethin' which might not be important but then again it might. It's been botherin' me and....."

There was nothing that Susana liked better than a juicy piece of gossip and before Mrs. Hardy could finish she rushed out to signal to her sister extolling her to hurry.

Mrs. Hardy nervously attacked the counters with an old rag while both women waited for Cornelia who had to stop to admire the season's last roses.

"Really Cornelia, you didn't have to stop and smell every rose in the garden. Did you?" asked her sister reproachfully. "Go ahead Mrs. Hardy, now that Cornelia's here you can tell us what you saw. Does it have to do with you know what?"

At first, Cornelia sent the two women a puzzled look. Then intercepting Susana's facial signals, she smiled reassuringly at Mrs. Hardy.

Mrs. Hardy's feverish hands had by this time polished the counters to a gleaming brilliance. But with Cornelia's encouragement, she settled down to her customary chattiness.

"I'm sure it's really nothin' important," she began, "But it has been on my mind since the murder and I don't feel comfortable tellin' that Scotland Yard Inspector somethin' that might not prove to be anythin'."

Cornelia tried to look grave and nodded assent while suppressing an urge to scream at the woman to get to the point.

Relishing the role of storyteller, the vicarage housekeeper/cook took a deep breath. "A week before the murder, I happened to be lookin' out the window as I washed the dinner pots and pans – *she* liked to have her dinner late – '*continental*' she called it. I'd have the table all set for their meal and then wash the dishes the next mornin'. Well what do you think I saw that evenin'?" She paused for effect.

Susana's wide-eyed face was within inches of Mrs. Hardy's in total fascination. Cornelia was digging the nails of her right hand into the palm of her left in exasperation. "I'm sure we have no idea," she prompted.

"I saw Miss Peters talkin' to someone – don't

ask me if it was man or woman, but sure as sure they were getting' an earful!" replied Mrs. Hardy with a firm nod of her head.

"Here in the shed?" asked Susana trying hard not to have school-girl giggles.

"Yep, that's right," Mrs. Hardy's mouth closed in a tight thin line.

"How could you see anything? Did they have the lights on?" asked Cornelia avoiding looking at Susana.

Mrs. Hardy made a vexed sound with her tongue. "O'course not. First of all, there's no electricity in here. Second of all, they were standin' right in front of the window and since I have to be home to feed my husband, it was still light out when I was at the kitchen sink. I could see them arguin' for a long time."

"How did you know they were arguing and are you sure you couldn't tell the gender of the other person?" asked Cornelia.

Shaking her head sadly Mrs. Hardy gave Cornelia a mournful look. "She was givin' whoever was fool enough to meet her here a piece of her mind. I'm tryin' to remember but for the life of me I can't be sure if it was man or woman. They were wearin' a heavy car coat and had a kind of cap on their head."

"How long were they in here?" asked Cornelia. She wished that this woman who seemed to be full of information on the whereabouts of people could have paid closer attention that evening.

"Oh I couldn't rightly say. I was rushing to finish the pots so's I could get home to give my man his dinner. I didn't really pay much attention to them. I finished my work, said goodnight to the vicar who was in his study, and left. O'course, if I'd known that she'd soon be murdered I might have paid closer attention."

"Dear me, I feel sorry for whoever was in here with Julia. Don't you?" observed Susana, then with a sideways glance at Mrs. Hardy added, "Of course I also feel badly that Julia's dead. But she did have a way with words that stung more than a slap on the face. Didn't she?" observed Susana.

Mrs. Hardy gave an amused howl then said, "I've been on the receivin' end of her verbal abuse many a time. I soon learned to treat it like water off a duck's back. But her attacks on the vicar made my blood boil and I'd stand up to her. Let her try that with me! There was no love lost between us, I can tell you!"

"I'm surprised you're still working here!" chuckled Cornelia.

"Oh she sacked me countless times. But the vicar refused to let me go. Only times he stood up to her. Funny isn't it?" and with that parting statement Mrs. Hardy ran out to attend the chicken which was roasting in the kitchen oven.

Chapter 24

When Sergeant Rogers phoned Larkspur Cottage regarding an interview after finding out that the Leslie sisters had lunched with it's occupants on the day of Betty's assault, he and the Inspector were enthusiastically invited for that same evening.

Larkspur Cottage was an attractive two over two bungalow set on a tiny lot with immaculately groomed landscaping. Three tall elm trees, planted on three sides gave the bungalow a protected air. It had been built in the nineteenth century on a small street intersecting the village green and it took its name from the Larkspurs that hugged the front of the house. When the police officers arrived, Debra and Phyllis were sitting on the front porch with a pitcher of martinis on a side table.

As the Scotland Yard men came up the tiny walkway, a large black cat came over to Rogers and wound around his legs. "Hello Churchill, how you doin'?" greeted the younger man bending down to pet the animal. Inspector Bunson, hurried up the couple of steps to the porch while pulling out a handkerchief.

"Don't tell us, you're allergic to cats, Inspector!" laughed Phyllis. Addressing Rogers she said, "Put Churchill inside will you Mike? Now that that's taken care of what would you like to drink,

Inspector? Debra is drinking a lime martini. I personally prefer a scotch and soda. We have a full bar and we can make you anything you'd like. Here's your martini Mike, nice and dry, one cocktail onion."

With a scotch and soda safely in his hands, Inspector Bunson sat comfortably back and looked around at the green landscape that was already changing into its gold and red autumn colors. "Your house must stay nice and cool during the summer heat, the trees are glorious."

"They're grand, aren't they? They give us a lot of shade but whoever planted them made sure that the larkspurs remain in more or less full sun. Which is a good thing because they make a spectacular show starting in spring and running almost into August," remarked Debra noting the inspector's interest.

"You didn't plant them?" asked an incredulous inspector.

"No, when we bought the place about fifteen years ago the owner gave us a little history of the place. It's always been known as Larkspur Cottage and even though the flowers are annuals they're very easy to grow. They can be seeded or divided and they hybridize on their own so every season we have a mixture of blue, white, violet, red and everything in between. It can be very lovely."

"Debra you're much too eager to leave out the distasteful attributes of anything or anyone!" interjected Phyllis with a laugh. "Inspector, those lovely looking stems are full of poisonous alkaloids which can kill a large mammal."

"Does Churchill know that?" asked Rogers mockingly.

"He worried us at first but he's remained true to his primal instincts and won't touch anything that's not meat. He's a carnivorous little beast," replied Phyllis with a wry smile.

"Sounds like Churchill and Jasper would make great buddies," kidded the Inspector over the last sip of his drink. Setting his glass down and assuming a more serious tone, he said, "I'm sorry to have to bring up a disagreeable topic in such pleasant surroundings but I'm afraid we must get on with our investigation."

Picking up his cue, Sergeant Rogers put his glass down and placed his laptop on the table. "We learned that you and the Leslie sisters had lunch together on the day Betty Smith was found in Hunter's Bosk. Is it possible to give us a rundown of where you were that day?"

The two women instinctively glanced at each other and then Phyllis spoke in a joking tone, "Well you're going to be very disappointed Inspector, as Mike can tell you, we lead a very boring existence really. We're more or less homebodies, Debra writes her children's books and I carry on with school and library duties."

Debra was quick to add, "But we're not total hermits, Inspector. We hike quite a lot around these parts and of course we do enjoy our bridge parties."

"As do many of our neighbors!" chortled Phyllis. "But as for the morning before our lunch with the Leslie girls, I'm sure we were sitting right where we are now enjoying coffee and the paper. I remember that Jim McCarthy had a whopper of an article about the motive in Julia's death. This is the biggest story he's had to cover since he started the paper and it's surprising what a good job he's doing. In fact I'm sure we're not the only ones in the village or town who look forward with morbid curiosity for his latest account."

"Yeah, he's actually a talented writer," observed Sergeant Rogers.

"Except for that bit about the motive," murmured a still riled Inspector Bunson. "About what time did you leave the house and did you stop anywhere before getting to the teashop?"

"Let's see, we decided to ride our bikes to the Tarts and Buns – really what a name, I have to laugh every time I say it – we were going to take a ride after lunch. The food's so good there that I really indulge so I like to put in a little exercise either before or afterwards. It only takes a couple of minutes by bike to get to the teashop so we must have left around ten minutes to two. We met the Leslies just as we were going inside," explained Debra.

Phyllis chuckled in recollection, "Poor Susana was all pink and out of breath. You know Cornelia and her health kicks."

"I believe they said you stayed in the teashop until about two o'clock. Would that be about right?" asked the Rogers.

"Yes, that's right. I spent some time at the counter choosing some pastries to bring home. Silly of me because I'd forgotten that we had our bikes and were planning to take a ride," said Debra.

"So instead, we loaded the bicycle baskets with the baked goods and took a short ride through the lane in the woods that runs to Mont Vernon and turned around and came back home. The entire ride must have taken no more than one hour," explained Phyllis.

"Would you say you got back here about four thirty?" asked Sergeant Rogers looking up from his computer.

"Thereabouts," replied Phyllis "We were having the 'Friends of the Library' over for drinks and hors d'ouvres at six so we just hung out here 'til then. By the time the last guest left it was close to nine and we were too tired to cook dinner so we polished off what was left of the hors d'ouvres and ate the pastries for dessert."

"Did you see anything or hear anything which might have looked out of place? As I'm sure I don't need to tell you, you were very close to the crime scene," said the inspector looking uncomfortable.

Again, the women exchanged looks. Debra shook her head with an expression of fear mixed with disgust while Phyllis looked straight at the Inspector and said, "We abhor any form of violence, Inspector. If we had seen anything which might have attracted our attention we would not have hesitated to notify the authorities."

Judging that they had received as much information as could be given, the police officers thanked the women and headed back to the station after first obliging their hosts with much sought after news on the condition of Betty Smith.

In the police car Inspector Bunson sat quietly looking out the window in the remaining daylight. The car passed the long green which was bordered by quaint eighteenth century homes, the stately church with the tall spire, atop which rested a copper weathervane in the shape of a hen, the vicarage, elementary school, town hall, some shops and the village library. He paid particular attention to the houses, the newest from the nineteenth century and marveled at how well maintained they all were and looked wistfully at their immaculately tended gardens.

"It's amazing how none of the houses look the same. I think that's what's so appealing, the fact that they all have their own character both in structure and landscape unlike the 'villas' found in the London suburbs," pronounced the inspector admiring the scenery.

Sergeant Rogers, who knew not to barge into the Inspector's thoughts when he was in his pensive mood, readily agreed. "Yeah, I guess having lived in the city all your life Epping's gotta seem idyllic. The natives certainly are a different breed and that's coming from someone who knows! Of course we do have the incomers, people like Debra and Phyllis, who give the place a little more aestheticism - they help 'distill' the waters if you will. Otherwise the village would be full of Jenkins'," expounded the Rogers.

"Did you say aestheticism? And can you explain what that word means? or did you hear it on one of those weird T.V. shows you watch?"

"It means culture, urbanity, fashion. Really, Inspector don't tell me you don't find those two women a little out of the common for our village?"

"Frankly, they do seem out of place in a small village. They're more the highbrow university types. I don't know quite what to make of Phyllis. She seems the type who could be ruthless if pushed," replied the Chief Inspector.

"That's Phyllis alright. If she doesn't like you, you'd better watch out. It doesn't matter who you are, she'll tell you what she thinks of you," replied Rogers. On the other hand, if she does like you, there's no better or loyal friend.

"Hmm, she was fast to chide Debra about the

poison in those flowers."

"Oh that's just because Phyllis has a doctorate degree in chemistry," replied the Sergeant in a matter of fact tone.

Inspector Bunson did a double take. "Well thank you for the information Sergeant! Don't you think that might have some bearing in a case of death by poison?" he asked in disbelief.

"Phyllis? Nah, I'll grant you she sometimes looks capable of murder, especially if you've ticked her off and as you said, she'll give a good verbal lashing, but actual murder? I don't think so."

Chapter 25

That evening, owing to Pinkey's night off, the Leslie siblings decided to have dinner at the Raven's Roost. The pleasantly sunny autumn day had changed to a cold blustery evening and by the dinner hour a slanting rain was coming down.

"Oh, I do like the rain! It makes everything so cozy doesn't it?" gabbed Susana quickly getting into the Rover.

"The only reason you like rain is because Cornelia can't make us walk when it's pouring," chided Jack as he slipped into the driver's seat.

"Oh be quiet you two. We actually could have walked if we hadn't had to wait so long for Billy Jenkins to take over standing guard at Martha's door. By the time he got to the house it had already started raining. The village constabulary must really be in dire straits if they have to depend on Jenkins to do anything," said Cornelia irritably.

"More to the point is whether our house will still be standing with two Jenkins' there alone!" laughed Jack.

"Pinkey offered to stay late but she had mentioned earlier that she was going to the movies with a young man from town so I couldn't ask her to stay. Could I?" replied Susana with dismay.

"Not to worry. Before she left Pinkey took a dinner tray in to Martha with the sedative Dr. Goodman ordered and mixed it into her tea and with all the food you left on the kitchen table for Jenkins, believe me, they'll both be asleep in less than one hour. On a different note, we need to go over the things we learned today while at the vicarage – of course we'll have to wait 'til we get home."

"Been snooping around have you? Come on girls, isn't it enough that we've had a murder right under our noses and now Betty is in hospital because some lunatic coshed her over the head? Do you want to be the next victims?" asked Jack looking over at Cornelia.

"Oh Jack don't talk like that, especially on a night like tonight. You're giving me the creeps. Isn't he Cornelia?" responded Susana.

"Hey, I thought you liked evenings like tonight?" smiled Jack looking in the rearview mirror at his sister. "All kidding aside, you both have to be a little more careful. There's someone out there who's already killed once and it looks like he or she's not afraid to do it again. I want you to promise me that you're not going to go around the village asking a lot of silly questions about which you know nothing."

"Oh that's fine by me, I'll be happy to take an oath. Won't you Cornelia?"

Cornelia was spared answering Susana because at that moment the car quickly swerved to the right and then came to a dead stop.. Both women began to scream at the top of their voices at their brother. "Talking of killing people! What kind of driving was that?" questioned Cornelia.

"Jack, really, how many times have I told you to stop driving like a maniac?" asked Susana.

211

"You girls have no appreciation for my masterful driving technique. Did you see how I beat out that guy for the only remaining parking space? You would have been forced to walk in the rain if it hadn't been for my skill!"

Inside the Raven's Roost the bar was doing a brisk business. It was customary for the locals to go to the pub directly after dinner so the pub was usually packed by eight o'clock at night. As the Leslies walked in friendly greetings were exchanged. Jack was able to find a booth for them that was just being cleared. Cornelia and Susana made themselves comfortable in the high backed seats that almost completely enclosed the occupants while Jack politely chatted with the men at the bar. After a few minutes he made his way to the booth carrying drinks followed by Jim McCarthy, who seemed to be very popular with the locals.

"Hullo Jim, come to join us?" greeted Cornelia.

"Yes, thanks. I've had to turn down at least half a dozen offers of beer since I walked in about twenty minutes ago! Funny how people think the press is privy to every scrap of information obtained by the police. I'm lucky to have gotten as much as I have!" replied the newspaperman sitting down next to Cornelia. "It's eery first Julia and now the vicious attack on Betty Smith."

"Please, you're talking to deaf ears, I bet you've had record sales these past few days with your coverage of the gruesome events. You can't fool us, Jim McCarthy. You're loving every second of it! Why it's a fight every morning to see whose going to get the paper - you know how we villagers love anything ghoulish!" rejoined Cornelia.

"I agree, it's been mesmerizing reading Jim!" exclaimed Susana taking a sip of her Gimlet cocktail, "Of course, I do pretend that I'm reading a fictional novel when I read your stories. It's frightening how these things are happening right in our midst. Isn't it?"

Changing his playful tone, the editor replied somberly, "Yeah, tough what happened to Betty Smith. I hear she's still in a coma and they don't know when she'll come out."

The Leslie siblings had purposely avoided speaking about Betty and the sudden mention of the attack caused an embarrassing pause in the conversation as the sisters quicky looked at their brother while Jack stared off in the distance. The silence was broken by the arrival at the table of Bert Colby proudly announcing the evening's dinner specials prepared by his wife, a garrulous bleached blonde who had begun her employment as the pub's barmaid.

Although the Leslies were all familiar with the pub's 'specials' which consisted of toned down, Anglicized versions of Italian favorites, they listened politely and ordered the traditional English fare, which if truth be told, tasted far better.

During dinner the conversation continued on the topic most on the minds of everyone. "I've been meaning to ask you about Martha Jenkins' escapade in Hunter's Bosk. I believe she was in the area where B...er... the attack took place. I've tried calling at her sister's place but they say she's not staying with them. I'd love to get an interview with her," said Jim.

"How did you know she was in those woods? I don't think I read a story about it in your paper. Did you learn that from the police?" asked Jack.

The editor gave an amused smile, "I know I'm just a country reporter but I still have my informants."

"Oh, of course – Constable Jenkins," sighed Cornelia.

"Hold on a minute! That's confidential information!" kidded Jim with a smile.

Jack, who was working on his second glass of beer broke in, "Ah yes, and you probably have access to the minutes of town meetings - all public records which are easily accessible."

"That's true, which brings me to a question. Were you aware that Sam Taylor had petitioned the town to have a portion of his land changed for use other than agriculture? And is it true that he had asked you if you'd be willing to sell him the parcel of land which you eventually donated to the town?"

"Certainly," replied Jack, "And a couple of days, later that old battle axe, Julia, called on us – during dinner mind you – asking us to donate the land to the town! Is that a coincidence or wha...hiccup."

"Jack, you talk too much!" exclaimed Cornelia reprovingly.

"Jim, you're not going to print that in your paper are you?" pleaded Susana.

Jim smiled and said, "Not at this time, Susana. But please try to understand that it's part of my job to follow up on leads."

Chapter 26

"Good grief, it's a good thing he was able to walk up the stairs or he'd have had to sleep on the library sofa," whispered Cornelia as she stood in the upstairs hall slumping against Jack's closed bedroom door.

Susana, who was resting on a small settee next to the door replied, "Ha! He's lucky we brought the car or he'd still be at the Raven's Roost. That boy never could hold his liquor. Imagine, completely blotto on four pints of beer!

Isn't it disgraceful?" Getting up and turning to look down the banister she continued, "Amazing how those Jenkins' can sleep. To think that with Jack singing his way up the stairs and with all our shushing to keep him quiet the 'pride of the constabulary' would have woken - is he snoring?"

"Of course Jenkins is snoring – he's on the job isn't he? Oh well, there goes our family pow-wow. I guess we'll just have to carry on by ourselves, Susana."

Susana shrugged her shoulders, "Just as well. Jack was already peeved with us because we did a little harmless snooping around the village. And anyway, he'd probably just laugh at us and tell us we're being 'dramatic' like he always does. He's a nice boy but he does get on my nerves." Susana stopped and cocked her head to one side. "Listen, the wind's starting to kick up. It's time to put the down comforters on the beds. Let's go make our Ovaltine then we can get on with our conference and I think there's some banana-nut bread left over from yesterday's tea too. Isn't it a perfect night to discuss the you know what?"

Having gotten their Ovaltine and changed into their pajamas, the sisters settled themselves comfortably in Susana's room to begin the discussion.

"Mmm, this banana-nut bread is positively delish! Pinkey's really becoming a first rate cook. Isn't she?" said Susana plumping her pillows and leaning back with a contented sigh.

Cornelia didn't respond. Curled up on the divan, she sat poised with her laptop. "Let's see, it's best to go about this in a methodical fashion. We should begin by listing everything we know about Julia." She typed '*JULIA*' at the top of the page in large bold letters.

"That's easy, the first item should be that she was the bossiest person on the planet. She had to give orders to everyone and she'd get so insulted if anyone dared try to oppose her. Right?" said Susana.

"Right. She was president of almost every committee and her every wish was her command. She was inconsiderate and unkind. She didn't care a hoot about people's feelings. Also, she was patronizing and condescending."

"She did not appreciate being contradicted and she'd let you now it. She was selfish, couldn't bare to have anyone in any position of authority – other than herself and she never said anything complimentary to or about anyone. In fact she was always derogatory.

Oh dear, I think we're speaking ill of the dead. Maybe we shouldn't be doing this?" observed Susana with a frown.

"Oh fiddlesticks," added Cornelia. Then using a little psychology on Susana she continued, "Shouldn't we be trying to help Mikey's future with Scotland Yard by finding Julia's murderer? We know he's a bright fellow but we don't know anything about the Inspector and if he's anything like our constabulary, Mike is going to need all the help he can get. Someone killed her because of what she said or did and if we write down her attributes, or lack thereof, we might come up with a clue that might catch the kil…perpetrator!," responded Cornelia.

"Ugh, but it's going to be such a long list! Did you finish your cake?"

"Yes, it was excellent. I might go down to the kitchen for more in a minute. Now let's continue we're on a roll."

"Okay, well, I believe she was envious. I mean all those times when someone would bring a gorgeous bouquet for the church or said something witty or had some special talent, Julia would say something snide with a horrid grimace on her face. I think she thought we were all fooled into believing it was a smile. She really was mean-spirited wasn't she?"

"Alright, we have something of a list. At least it's a start." said Cornelia turning the laptop screen towards her sister.

JULIA
BOSSY
INCONSIDERATE
UNKIND
PATRONIZING
CONDESCENDING
SELSFISH
DERROGATORY
HATEFUL
MEANSPIRITED
CONTROLLING
DEVIOUS

"Great, now let's go down and get another slice of banana-nut bread. After all, if you expect me to be Beth to your Nancy, I'll need more sustenance. And instead of Ovaltine, I'm going to brew up a pot of strong coffee. I have a feeling we're going to be up all night. Aren't we?" replied Susana, "Ooh, listen to that wind! I imagine that by morning the lawns will be covered in leaves. Don't you love this time of year?"

Having replenished their midnight snack the sisters were back in Susana's room ready to continue the discussion.

"At this point we should include facts which might be pertinent or could have led to Julia being murdered," remarked Cornelia fussing with her laptop.

"Do you really think we might find something useful for the police?" asked Susana with a skeptical look.

"Of course. We're insiders! Haven't you noticed how the villagers never hesitate to tell us things? People tend to be suspicious of the police.

They would never converse with them in the same manner that they do with us. Now let's get down to business." Cornelia typed the title.

'PERTINENT FACTS'

"Let's begin with the fact that Sam Taylor was the person who first approached us about the business of land. He contacted us with an offer of purchasing the parcel abutting the church," wrote Cornelia.

"I remember he told us he was going to start some sort of business and needed to use all the land bordering our properties. Right?"

"Correct. Didn't Jim say that Sam had also applied for a change of property use at town hall? Sam Taylor owns a big piece of land and with the economic market in the depressed state it's in I'd be willing to say that farming isn't exactly bringing in the big bucks. Also, and this is important, let's not forget that just a few days later Julia asked us if we'd be willing to donate that same parcel to the town to extend the cemetery. Why even then we thought the coincidence strange."

"Cornelia, I just thought of something!" uttered Susana in a stage whisper. "Could Sam and Julia have had a romantic interest?" Seeing Cornelia's face change into a look of disgust, she continued in her normal voice. "No really, it could happen. We know that Julia was always making goo-goo eyes at him and that he was always trying to avoid her. We all know she was incredibly persistent when she wanted something. Maybe he just gave up trying to escape her ardent advances – are we really talking about Julia?"

"Oh brother! Talk about Nancy Drew! Come

on, you're not as dumb as Beth," replied an amused Cornelia. "But as we've said, the fact that both Julia and Sam approached us about the same piece of land is peculiar and Julia's motives had to have been selfish, egocentric and/or malicious or all of the above. She might possibly have been trying to block any attempt on his part to obtain that land. Hm, there might possibly be a tie there somewhere." contemplated Cornelia.

"Yep, and don't forget controlling, mean, and envious. This reminds me of when we were in school and used to gossip about the girls we couldn't stand and the boys on whom we had crushes, Fun isn't it?" declared Susana.

"You're right, things haven't changed – you're still as flighty as you were then. Can you please try to keep your mind on the topic?"

"Alright, alright. Hey, I've got a good one! Do you remember that two years ago the vicar and Julia went on vacation to the Riviera and when they came back she told everyone that the Riviera was a place of debauchery full of morally depraved winos? I can still see her face all pious and self-righteous saying 'Sooo much sun and skin!' Didn't we almost die laughing? Jack still makes me laugh imitating her. Remember?" recalled Susana in-between peals of laughter.

Cornelia was unable to reply due to the fact that she was also having difficulty breathing. Holding her sides as she laughed she implored her sister, "S-t-o-p...I can't...breathe!"

"Or maybe she just said those things when she really was one of the bathing beauties on the beach soaking in the sun in a topless bikini! Can you picture her? She'd look just like a plucked chicken –

especially those legs! I can't believe I'm saying these things – can you?" laughed Susana.

"Heavens, that was hysterical," replied a weak Cornelia as she wiped away tears of laughter. "No more joking Susana. What about the relationship between the vicar and his sister? I mean it's pretty terrible to be thinking that a servant of the church would murder anyone let alone his own sister. But if we're going to do this correctly then we have to look at everyone and everything objectively."

"I agree but it's not very nice. But I suppose that just because Reverend Peters is a Church of England priest does not necessarily absolve him from committing murder. Oh, but it's too horrible to contemplate isn't it?" Frowning, Susana took a sip of her Ovaltine and said, "We're getting ahead of ourselves, we were listing pertinent facts and these are only conjectures. Aren't they?" Not waiting for her sister's answer, she continued in a quavering voice, "Oh dear, I just remembered something. When we were inside the garden shed at the vicarage I happened to notice a small box of strychnine in a corner - that's bad, isn't it?"

Cornelia turned white as a sheet and stared at her sister. After a few seconds she said faintly, "I suppose you're sure it was actually strychnine and not something else?"

"Well I certainly didn't taste it to fine out! Should I have?" replied her sister.

"We have to put that down as a fact – it's used in gardens to keep pests away," said Cornelia sounding hopeful.

Eager to change the subject, Susana said, "And what about Julia's going up to London once a month? Do you remember Mrs. Hardy and the vicar

222

corroborating Julia's trips? Really! Do you really believe she was going there for artistic erudition?"

"It does seem somewhat extravagant to go up that often. But she did have independent means."

Leaning back on her pillow after pouring herself another cup of coffee Susana contemplated, "If you ask me, she had something going on there. Do you suppose she was the head of some kind of illicit operation? I've read about things like that, you know. Let me think," she screwed up her eyes to the ceiling, tapped her chin with her finger and said, "I've got it! She ran a high-class brothel! Amazing isn't it?"

"Julia – a *'madam'*?" asked Cornelia astonished at her sister's flights of fancy. "Really Susana, anything's possible but Julia in the role of a 'madam' is beyond crazy."

"Well if it's so crazy what about Mrs. Hardy's story about seeing Julia in the shed at night talking to someone?"

"Now that is relevant. But you don't really expect me to believe that this person was a 'client' of hers and that the shed was her Epping office do you? It's too ridiculous for words! In fact it's hysterical! I will give you that it was probably a clandestine meeting and that's definitely information for the police. So long as we're talking about Mrs. Hardy's observations we should also take into account the fact that Julia was a domineering sister who controlled her brother with an iron fist."

"Yes and don't forget that she tried to sack Mrs. Hardy just like she sacked the dozens of other housekeepers before her. Or did they quit on their own? Oh my gosh, do we have to count them as suspects too?"

"Susana, if you were Julia's housekeeper how

long do you think you'd last? What with her ridiculous exigencies not to mention her nasty disposition, most likely the majority of the women quit of their own volition. And as far as motives go, anyone who ever met Julia probably had a good one. Unfortunately we don't have the resources of Scotland Yard to help us so we have to concentrate our investigation on our fellow citizens of Epping."

"If I was in Julia's employment I might have seriously contemplated poison as a form of suicide. And the way she treated her brother! That's something else. Imagine, depriving him of food!" Susana shivered and pulled the covers more closely around her, "Somehow I can't help but feel that whoever poisoned her actually did the community a service. Isn't that evil of me?"

"Actually, I was thinking the same thing and if truth be told, our sentiments are probably held by the entire village. But the fact that Betty was brutally attacked has made things more complicated," said Cornelia with a sigh.

"I'm afraid it keeps pointing to a homicidal maniac doesn't it?" asked Susana looking guardedly at the windows.

"Hm, and don't forget that Martha was pushed down our cellar stairs on the night of Julia's death. There's a connection there somewhere. Of course it would help if Martha would act normally for once and give the police a detailed report."

"Oh Cornelia, you know that Martha is as batty as they come! She's always touting her 'second sight' and that things 'come' to her. Maybe it's just a coincidence that she was here when Julia died and passing through Hunter's Bosk when Betty was attacked or maybe it's her psychic powers..." Susana stopped midstream with a look of horror, "Uh, oh, you don't suppose we have a cold-blooded killer under our roof do you?" she asked in a stage whisper.

"No I don't but in any case she's locked in her room with a constable on guard – even if he is related to her. Good night, Susana. I should think the Inspector should be very pleased when he hears what we've done. By the way, I intend to sleep until lunchtime tomorrow," said Cornelia heading out the door.

"Good night – maybe we should lock our bedroom doors?" replied her sister from under the covers.

Chapter 27

Early the following morning, Cornelia's wish to sleep in was disturbed by a loud ruckus coming from downstairs. She lay quietly with one eye opened trying to determine if she was dreaming. Just as she had decided that the noises were primarily Martha's screeching accompanied by intermittent male voices, there was a knock at her door and in rushed Pinkey waving the morning paper.

"Oh Mrs. C., Auntie Martha's screaming her head off!" she declared somewhat unnecessarily. Then more to the point she continued, "When I went in with her breakfast, cousin Billy had told her that Ms. Smith had died during the night and that's completely set her off. Uncle Billy called for the Inspector and Sergeant Rogers and they're with her now. They're asking if you wouldn't mind speaking with them when they've finished."

Cornelia sat up in bed now completely awake from the shock of the latest news.

"It's unbelievable...the poor girl. I'm stunned, I don't know what to think."

Pinkey held the newspaper up to Cornelia. "Uncle Billy got it all wrong, Mrs. C. There hasn't really been another death – yet. The doctors just say that it's likely that Ms. Smith will never come out of the coma. It's all here in the paper. If she does die, that will make two people murdered right here in our village."

Putting on her robe, Cornelia headed for her brother's room only to find that he wasn't there. She found Jack and Susana in the library. Susana, nervously winding and unwinding a handkerchief, was seated in front of the fireplace watching her brother's ministrations with the fire-logs. Neither was speaking.

"I'm terribly sorry Jack, I guess you've already heard," spoke Cornelia.

Without turning around, Jack answered, "The Inspector phoned me at daybreak."

After their interview with Martha, Inspector Bunson and Sergeant Rogers informed Cornelia that having been frightened into hysterics from the inaccurate news of Betty's death, Martha had agreed to voluntarily tell her story of what she had seen and heard on the evening of the young woman's brutal attack. However she maintained that she would not set foot outside of the manor until the killer had been apprehended.

Now more eager than ever to assist the police, Cornelia requested from a stupefied Inspector Bunson and an equally flabbergasted Sergeant Rogers that a meeting take place wherein the two women could go over their findings. Inspector Bunson, no longer surprised at the comportment of the residents of Epping, resigned himself to his fate and readily capitulated to meet with the ladies later that afternoon at the police station.

Upon leaving Blandings, a weary Inspector Bunson and the ever-energetic Rogers headed for the Tarts and Buns for breakfast. Even at that early hour, the news of Betty's prognosis was the prime topic of conversation in the village. Behind the counter a slight altercation ensued between Ginny and Liz as to who would have the honor of escorting the now embarrassed officers to a table. It was amicably decided that one would show them to a table while the other followed with the menus. Having accomplished their united mission, both young women remained transfixed at a nearby alcove in the expectation of catching any snippet which later could be felicitously conveyed to less fortunate ears. Rogers, who was used to this type of behavior from young women smiled charmingly at them producing bashful giggles.

Suffering from lack of sleep the Inspector looked at the day's menu, asked his Sergeant to place an order of hot oatmeal and coffee for him then got up to go to the men's room. When he returned, he noticed that the young women were no longer near the table and neither was Sergeant Rogers.

"If Rogers has better things to do than eat breakfast, which I doubt, I'm not going to waste my time looking for him," mused a weary Inspector Bunson.

Just as he took his seat, Ginny, now without Liz who was forced to attend to other customers, appeared carrying a bowl of hot oatmeal and a pot of coffee. "Sergeant Rogers went outside to take a phone call. He said to go ahead and start without him," said Ginny directing a searching gaze at the front windows.

Inspector Bunson nodded knowingly and began pouring heavy cream and cinnamon on his oatmeal.

"Sorry, but I had no choice," whispered

Sergeant Rogers quickly slipping into his seat, "Once you left they felt it was safe to question me about the 'gory murders'. I kept telling them that I couldn't talk about the case but they wouldn't believe me. It was like they were giving me the third degree! Finally, I got a call from the Yard and I used that as an excuse to escape. Phew – please don't leave me alone with them again!"

The Sergeant's woes changed the Inspector's depressed mood and he actually enjoyed his oatmeal. When Liz came to the table carrying a tray heavily laden with Roger's enormous order. His senior officer longingly eyed the bacon however his attempt to serve himself a slice from the platter was foiled when the Sergeant deftly slid the entire contents onto his plate forcing the Inspector to place a separate order for himself.

In his customary manner, Sergeant Rogers ate with gusto quickly finishing off a plate of the English 'Bubble and Squeak' and then setting forth on a plate of eggs with a side of rashers. The Inspector, for once not succumbing to his bilious attacks, also ate with relish.

"Don't look now but the vigil has resumed at four o'clock," whispered the Sergeant. "I feel like a monkey at the zoo the way they watch me eat my breakfast."

Inspector Bunson chuckled and with good humor said, "That's a very good comparison, Sergeant. I knew there was something familiar about the way you eat."

Immune to the barb, the Rogers responded, "It's just that you don't know how to savor the food you eat. You don't appreciate the different flavors or textures. It's an art you know," and with that he picked up another slice of fried bread, mopped the runny eggs with the bread, and placed the tidbit in his mouth with a satisfied sigh.

Unfortunately for the Inspector, this last display of gourmet appreciation affected his delicate constitution and he rapidly turned a pale shade of green. Quickly reaching for his coat pocket, he pulled out his antacids and popped a handful into his mouth. Not waiting for the check, he grabbed a napkin and made a mad dash for the exit.

Once outside, the brisk fall air served to revive his discomfiture and with Sergeant Rogers on his heels, he headed for the parked car taking in
large gasps of air while flapping his arms to his chest much to the amusement of the younger man.

The ride to the station was made in silence as the Sergeant, by way of sidelong glances noticed his chief's twitching nose.

Arriving at the police station, the two men were informed that the Chief Constable was looking forward to meeting with them after lunch to discuss the latest developments in the case.

"Has Martha always been like that?" asked the Inspector after they had been at their desks for a while.

"If you mean 'daft', the answer is in the affirmative. Screwiness runs in that family and if you ask me, the Jenkins' take pride in their genetic abberation."

"Funny, Pinkey didn't strike me as being anything like her aunt," replied the Inspector.

"I know, must be a mutation," answered a distracted Sergeant Rogers still staring at his screen.

"Do you think Martha's facts are credible? If

we have to meet with the C.C. I don't want to go in there with a bunch of fabricated nonsense that will make us look like fools."

Getting up and walking to the window and looking at the autumn foliage the Sergeant didn't speak for a few minutes.

"She's too frightened to give us phony information. I mean she was knocked on the head and then pushed down the basement stairs – probably left for dead and she knows it. And let's not forget that according to her statement, she saw someone leaving the area of Hunter's Bosk the day Betty was accosted. She wants the killer apprehended."

"What about that Moe Stone character? I've seen his kind in the City. Somehow I don't see him as the country type." said the Inspector. Staring at his notes he continued, "His background check is okay, he came out from Manchester about twelve years ago. Runs a small used car lot out in Milford. Takes a role in village politics. Could be covering his tracks with his story that he heard a moan on his way home from the pub when he just happened to be walking through Hunter's Bosk. Shows some cunning if he's the murderer and thought that either someone saw him or that we might have found some evidence pointing to him."

"There's always been talk that he was Julia Peters' patsy. Voting anyway she told him. Maybe he got tired of the villagers talking behind his back and decided to get back at the culpable person. Might be some motive there," replied the Sergeant.

The Inspector looked at his watch and groaned, "If you're still hungry after that enormous breakfast, you'll have to run down to the cafeteria and bring back a sandwich. We're going to stay here and go through this list systematically before we talk to the C.C."

"No worries. For starters, we'll have to put the victim's closest relation at the top of the suspect list. And that would be none other than her brother, the much loved vicar," said the Sergeant with a mischievous grin "We know that he was a victim of domestic violence and that he suffered quietly for years. Sorry, but Julia Peters was a fiend of the first order and if the old guy finally took action, I certainly don't want to be the one to charge him."

Feeling old and weary Inspector Bunson shook his head in an effort to clear his mind and said, "There's plenty of motive there but I don't see him as having the temperament to do something like that. He must have used the abuse as a form of religious penance. Of course the unlikeliest people have been the foulest and most callous of killers. So unfortunately for him and us, we have to keep him, as you say, 'at the top of the suspect list'."

The rest of the morning was spent going over statements and double-checking facts against evidence in preparation for the meeting with the Chief Constable. Inspector Bunson's mood continued somber and Sergeant Rogers' observation that the difficulty of the case lay in the fact that the crimes had taken place in a small country village where everyone was enmeshed in everyone else's affairs, did nothing to raise his spirits.

In a rare show of temper, he burst out, "I'm so fed up with this case I wouldn't mind rounding up the entire bunch and placing them all under arrest!"

Major Geoffrey Sandowne, retired military, dearly loved his native village and was very much liked and respected by his fellow residents, his keen intelligence, country common sense and military background prohibited him from any romantic notions about the human condition, rendering him well aware of the idiosyncrasies of his fellow residents. From the outset of the case his sympathies were with the Inspector who was unwittingly thrown into the meleé of everyday village life and forced to bring to the surface the culprit or culprits from a quagmire of characters. While Major Sandowne's requests to meet with his officers to discuss a case was a technical formality, he had early on set a precedent that his meetings were more a type of informal brainstorming rather than a one sided lecture on procedurals of successful investigations. This meeting followed the same course and by the time a constable interrupted the conference with a reminder to the C.C. that he was expected home by mid-afternoon to attend his granddaughter's ballet recital, all three men sensed that somewhere in that great morass of information, there was evidence, if not completely obvious, which would shift the focus from several suspects to one in particular.

    When the Scotland Yard detectives were alone in their office, Sergeant Rogers observed, "Interesting that the C.C. was excited about our meeting with the Ms. Leslies. I'm beginning to agree with him. I mean they've been around for an awfully long time and they're very friendly and well liked by the villagers and even though they live in the 'manor' they're looked upon same as everyone else. I mean they're not stand-offish and they participate in village affairs but they're not busy bodies like some other who'll remain nameless."

Chapter 28

At the manor the Leslie siblings sat in the dining room finishing their lunch. The sisters could barely contain themselves with anticipation of their meeting with the Scotland Yard detectives. Jack noticed that during the meal, Susana seemed unusually nervous and unsettled while Cornelia was chattier than ever.

"Okay girls, I can tell that something is up and I'd like to know what it is - you know – just for safety's sake."

"Really Jack, you sound as if Cornelia and I were up to something illegal! Or maybe you think one of us is the fiend behind these murders?" replied Susana hastily jabbing her spoon into the pumpkin custard and spraying the contents into her brother's face. "Oh dear, see what you've made me do?" she said holding a napkin to her face to hide her smile.

"I just want to know if you two are going to be playing detectives today. I don't want to find that I've got to either bail you out of jail or something worse," replied her brother ineffectually wiping custard from his face.

"Don't be an ass. We're not 'playing' at anything and as for being arrested I don't think Inspector Bunson is that stupid or creative," said

Cornelia. "By the way, what are your plans this afternoon?" she added trying to sound nonchalant.

"We'd like to know if *you're* doing anything we should know about?" added Susana defiantly.

Jack looked at both his sisters and sighed, "Alright, you win. I'm going to London to purchase a machete to use on my next victim." Seeing the color drain from his sisters' faces he quickly added, "You see? Now I hope you realize that you can't discount anyone as the possible murderer and if you know what's good for you you'll mind your own business and stay home where it's safe. I'm going into London on business but I should be back for dinner," and with that he kissed each of his sisters and left.

As soon as the dining room door closed, Susana began fanning herself with her napkin and with a feigned air said, "Oh my gosh, that was lucky! I thought I'd have to come up with some story – and you know how flustered and confused I get when I have to make up something on the spur of the moment – don't I?"

Cornelia also breathed a sigh of relief, "I don't know what got into me. I was yakking uncontrollably and half the time I had no idea what I was saying. And what about you Ms. Butterfingers? First you have the peas rolling all over the table and then you cover Jack with pumpkin custard! No wonder he was suspicious," replied her sister laughing.

Susana suddenly became serious. "I've just thought of something Cornelia. What if Jack finds out about our meeting with the detectives? Ohh, he'd be so angry, wouldn't he?"

"Why should he find out? Unless of course somebody were to let something slip..." Cornelia left the sentence unfinished for emphasis and gave her sister a questioning look.

Susana got up from the table and mechanically tugging at her pullover stood as erect as possible with her chin held high in an attempt to gain as much height as possible on her five foot frame. "If you're insinuating that I might accidentally give away the show Cornelia, then I must remind you that in the past it's been you who has failed in the acting department far more times than I." she replied with dignity.

"Oh let's not quibble now. It's time we started for the meeting. I'm going upstairs to get my laptop and then we can walk to the police station. Now be sure to put on your walking shoes!"

"Drat my walking shoes don't we have driving shoes anywhere?" replied Susana huffily.

Chapter 29

Sergeant Rogers sat at his desk no longer preoccupied with the notes in front of him. The conference with the Leslies was due to start in less than five minutes and there was no sign of his superior officer.

Chief Inspector Bunson had not been looking forward to this unprecedented meeting and it was now almost two hours since he had told the Sergeant that what he needed was a walk in the crisp autumn air. As the time for the meeting got closer, Rogers began wondering if the Inspector had possibly gotten himself lost or been in an accident. There was a popular country saying that limbs from trees in woods were 'widow makers' and the Sergeant fervently hoped the inspector had not gone wondering alone in the countryside.

Taking one last expectant glance out the window, the Sergeant was forced to acknowledge that he would have to conduct the conference alone.. It wasn't that he had any qualms about speaking with the Leslie sisters. After all, he had known them all his life. He was, in fact, eager to find out the quality and quantity of their information. His only concern was how he would guide the discussion without causing disrespect or insult to the two well-meaning ladies.

Hearing the Leslie's animated voices in the hall, Rogers automatically straightened his tie and passed a hand over his already neat hair. As he was about to clear his desk of the ever-present clutter he was greeted by non other than Inspector Bunson in the company of the Leslie sisters. His Sergeant's relieved expression was not lost on the Inspector as he ushered the ladies inside while explaining to the Sergeant that he had had the pleasure of running into the ladies as he was passing the manor drive. The three had come down to the center of the village and along the way he had learned some very interesting village folklore.

"Just giving the Inspector a little local color. Our village is so full of charm don't you agree Mikey?" remarked Susana chattily. Then not waiting to hear the officer's answer continued, "Yes, Epping is a special place and we must try to keep it that way. That's why it's so necessary that we find the maniac who's terrorizing the village. We can't have people afraid to walk out of their doors for fear of being murdered. It's dreadful! We've never had anything like this – have we?"

Inspector Bunson wondered if he would be forced to deal with hysterics and quickly asked if she'd like a glass of water.

"Don't mind Susana, Inspector she's a trifle longwinded. Although she's right when she says that the village is paralyzed with fear. That's why my sister and I have decided to do all we can to help Scotland Yard find the responsible party."

After a few moments of stunned silence, Inspector Bunson looked pleadingly at his Sergeant then turned to the sisters and replied with a weak smile, "That's very kind of you ladies."

Officer Rogers took the hint and banishing thoughts of hours of listening to two women's tales of village gossip, said, "Thank you, we certainly can use any help we can get! If you'll give me your information I'll put it into the computer."

"That's fine. We've been working on this for a few days ourselves and I've stored all of our findings in my laptop which I have right here!" replied Cornelia pulling out her laptop from her huge purse as if she were a magician pulling a rabbit out of a hat.

The sergeant's eyes brightened and he replied, "That's great! Why not forward all your information to me and that way the Inspector and I can go over your work this evening!"

Cornelia made a slight coughing noise, "No Mikey, you'll never be able to make heads or tails of my notes. They're really just outlines and bullet points. Susana and I hoped to discuss our findings with you and the Inspector. As we've said before, people speak more openly to locals than to Scotland Yard - especially villagers."

Inspector Bunson had been sitting at his desk quietly assessing the developments. He agreed with his C.C. that these two women, who were highly respected members of the community, could have obtained information that might otherwise never have come to light. True, it would probably be jumbled up with prejudice and gossip but he'd worry about that later.

"We're very grateful that you've taken it upon yourselves to offer to assist us and we'll be only too glad to have your very valuable cooperation. Before we begin would either of you ladies like tea or coffee?" Inspector Bunson tried his best to seem agreeable.

Susana gave a little shudder of excitement, "No thank you, Inspector, we really are so thrilled to be able to work with Scotland Yard! Imagine Cornelia, did you ever think we'd be assisting Scotland Yard with their investigations?"

From behind his computer screen Officer Rogers almost drew blood biting his lip.

Inspector Bunson privately thanked Providence that his London colleagues were miles away. He coughed, stalling for time, and then decided to face the consequences like a man. But first, he would get back at his Sergeant for cowering behind a computer screen. With some sarcasm he quipped, "Sergeant Rogers, I think it would be a good idea to give the Mrs. Leslies our full attention. We can input their contributions afterwards." This had the desired effect and Rogers peevishly closed his computer.

The women had been eagerly anticipating this moment and like thoroughbreds at the starting gate once they were given the green light there was no stopping them and both began to speak. Aware of the possibility that they might be considered meddling old ladies, they stopped, apologized and begged the other to continue.

To Susana's dismay, Cornelia accepted her offer. "I hope we haven't given you the impression that we're two busy-bodies taking up your valuable time Inspector. As we said earlier, Susana and I have obtained, what seem to us, curious details which perhaps might aid you in your investigations. I can assure you, Inspector, that neither my sister nor I have illusions of being undercover detectives nor did we purposely gather these facts with the intent to obstruct or impede your inquiries."

Susana could no longer remain in the background. "That's just it Inspector, we didn't go around the village probing and searching for clues. We live in the village and our observations happened in the course of our daily activities. Nothing more! Fortuitous, don't you agree?" she sat back smiling at her own and Cornelia's cleverness.

Meanwhile Rogers was doing his best to keep a straiaght face as he pictured the two dignified women whom he had known all his life surreptitiously hiding behind shrubbery while snooping around the village. Thinking things over he considered that no one least of all the villagers would remotely think that these ladies would involve themselves in undercover activities even though everyone knew of their eccentricity. After much thought he came to the conclusion that in fact they probably would be more successful than the police in gathering useful information.

"Yes, well," continued Cornelia, "we decided to base our efforts around the most significant person in this terrible affair. That, of course, is Julia. Mikey, you grew up in this village and I think you would agree that Julia had a very difficult nature. But because you're young and a bachelor, you really don't know the extent of her character."

The young officer raised his eyebrows and settled back for what he was sure would be something like the soap operas his girlfriends watched on the telly.

Starting to feel uncomfortable, Susana promptly added, "It's not that we enjoy speaking ill of the dead but with what has happened we have no choice. Julia was not a nice person. I'm sorry, but that's just the way it is. Cornelia and I made a list of her traits - believe me, they're not pretty. Are they Cornelia?"

"No, they're not. It would be perfectly appropriate as a list of the most odious attributes. Julia considered the village her kingdom and believed herself it's monarch. She had to have a hand in all village affairs and insisted on the chairmanship of all the committees. The residents of Epping are not ignorant country bumpkins no matter what Scotland Yard may think. They are peace loving, simple folk who would rather shy off an argument than rebel against their much loved vicar's sister."

"And she ruled those committees with an iron fist. If you didn't carry out her orders or got pre-approval for the least little thing she would let you have it." said Susana thoughtfully. Then furrowing her brow added, "Interesting how she never raised her voice or used foul language. She had a condescending and patronizing tone that she'd use to make you shrivel up and feel like an idiot. I'd shake like a leaf whenever she'd walk up to me even if I wasn't on one of her committees. Didn't I Cornelia?"

"She didn't like anyone gaining the upper hand in anything. Her attitude was that the village belonged to her! Added Cornelia."

"Almost pathological. Oh dear, we sound awful! But really, you can ask anyone in the village about Julia's ways - sad isn't it?" said Susana worriedly.

Inspector Bunson and Sergeant Rogers nodded in unison. Both men hoping that the 'conference' had come to an end.

"Thank you ladies, you have given us inval..." began the inspector but was not given a chance to finish.

"Oh but we're not in the least bit finished! We've only just started Inspector. Haven't we Cornelia?"

Cornelia, somewhat annoyed at the interruption, replied, "We're laying the foundation for what might be motives in the case, Inspector. You must see that Julia was a very loathesome person."

"You should hear what Mrs. Hardy, the vicarage housekeeper, told us! Goodness, she opened our eyes to another facet of Julia that we never knew existed. I mean we knew that the turnover of vicarage housekeepers could make your head spin but we never would have guessed about the vicar!" replied Susana. Then in a wistful tone added, "My, those shortbread cookies were delicious weren't they?"

Cornelia noticed the look that passed between the Scotland Yard men. Sensing a slight change in the detectives' attitude, she grinned inwardly and responded, "It seems that Julia carried the age old sibling rivalry to new heights Inspector. She was the elder of the two and according to Mrs. Hardy Julia never outgrew the childish use of birth order. Mrs. Hardy was very vocal about her feelings of the way Julia controlled her brother's life. While all of Epping was aware of Julia's habit of regulating everything in the village, I don't think anyone knew the extent of her domination over her brother. From what Mrs. Hardy said, I would go so far as to say that Julia enjoyed the power of overseeing her brothers everyday life to the point of subjugation."

"Did you know that Julia was in the habit of regularly going up to London for long weekends? Cornelia and I were shocked when we found that out. She was sooo...prudish about social behavior. She maintained that she was a teetotaler, you know. Well, she wouldn't allow her brother around! I'd like to know what she was up to if she didn't want her brother with her! Can you imagine?" declared Susana indignantly. Then almost immediately added as if to herself, "She was always very chummy with Moe Stone. Makes one wonder, doesn't it?"

The officers exchanged furtive glances. This was not what they had expected.

Confident that the officers were clinging to their every word, Cornelia continued. "As we stated earlier, Julia's bullying personality encompassed everything and everyone in Epping. And as you know from our statements, Sam Taylor had initially contacted us about buying a particular piece of land. At the time, we had no foreseeable use for the land and of course the extra money would undoubtedly have come in handy. But before we could meet with our attorney to discuss Sam's proposal, Julia contacted us begging that we donate that same piece of land to the village in order to extend the cemetery. It took us a while to decide but ultimately we opted to donate the land to the village. We found it curious that both Julia and Sam were interested in the same piece of land but we put it down to the village telegraph. Now we're not so sure."

At this point, the Leslie sisters had the complete attention of the Scotland Yard detectives and they gave each other knowing looks at the success of their endeavor.

"Yes, when you think about it, almost the entire village of Epping had a motive for doing away with Julia and I'm afraid it must be very easy to obtain poison. Why I saw a small bag of strychnine in the vicar's garden shed just the other day. And of course the woods are full of all sorts of poisonous plants. Aren't they?" said Susana absently.

"Are you sure it was strychnine you saw?" asked a bewildered Sergeant Rogers.

"Oh definitely. It was when Cornelia and I were walking in the vicarage rose garden and Mrs. Hardy was waving madly at us from the potting shed so of course we had to find out what she wanted. She was very agitated about something she had seen a few nights prior to Julia's death. Wasn't she, Cornelia?" Susana paused to take a much-needed breath although those who knew her would swear that it was a pause for dramatic effect. The Scotland Yard detectives willingly indulged her with marked expectancy.

"Well to go on, Mrs. Hardy had seen Julia in the potting shed with someone. Apparently Julia was very angry and berating the poor soul. Unfortunately, Mrs. Hardy couldn't tell if it was a male or female but they were definitely getting the brunt of Julia's wrath. I feel sorry for whomever it was, don't you?"

Overcoming his sense of speechlessness, the inspector replied admiringly, "I must say you ladies have certainly been able to gather quite a bit of information. I'm beginning to agree with you that people around here will tell you things that they conveniently forget or leave out when speaking to the police. In this respect did any of your...er...contacts, have any evidence of anyone in particular having a romantic relationship with Ms. Peters?"

Cornelia made a vexed sound with her tongue and replied, "Definitely not, Inspector. And I certainly can't think of anyone fitting that role. Can you Susana?"

In a desperate attempt to avoid the eyes of the police officers Susana responded by quickly getting up to stare out of the window while at the same time suppressing a desire to giggle. "The cold snap we've had has really had a wonderful effect on the fall colors, don't you think so?" she said feebly. Then without bothering to turn around she said in a faint tone as if to herself, "Oh dear, there might be something to what Mrs. Hardy saw. Makes one wonder doesn't it?"

The curiosity of the Scotland Yard detectives was now undoubtedly piqued and they both leaned towards the plump figure at the window straining to hear what she was saying. With growing interest the detectives asked the women to repeat Mrs. Hardy's story. By this time, it had been almost two and a half hours since the meeting had started by which time, the sisters rose from their chairs and thanked the Scotland Yard men for their courteous attention.

Needless to say, the officers were once again astonisheded at the information so easily obtained by the two women and with sincere cordiality they gave hearty proclamations of gratitude with requests that if they should gain any further information it would be the Yard's pleasure to consult with them.

As the two women were escorted to the door, Susana suddenly stopped and said, "By the way, the mallet to our dinner gong is missing. We've had to manage with a wooden spoon from the kitchen – doesn't quite sound the same, does it?"

Inspector Bunson and Sergeant Rogers returned to their office in complete silence. Both men still too dumbfounded over the unexpected results of their meeting.

With a sigh the Inspector broke the silence, "This village and its inhabitants are either going to push me over the edge or make me alter my approach to life."

Rogers smiled, "Told ya. Those two are pretty smart. They've given us a lot to digest. I have an inkling that there are things in there that could be tied together but I'm too tired to try to unravel them," he finished with a wide yawn.

It was decided that they would get a good night's rest and in the morning begin the job of trying to link all the pieces together.

Meanwhile, Cornelia and Susana spent an animated time walking home beaming with pride on a job well done. They jabbered about how they had managed to captivate Scotland Yard with their detecting and gleefully recounted the mesmerized looks on the faces of the professionals.

Upon arriving at Blandings, a worried Pinkey greeted them at the door, "Ooo I thought you were never coming home. I wanted to surprise you by making a French dessert for dinner. I've been working on it since this morning but it doesn't seem to want to cooperate. I've tried a couple of times already and I'm ready to quit but now that you're here maybe you can help me," she said looking hopefully at Susana.

Thinking that she'd really prefer to sit down after the walk from the station and have her tea, Susana smiled encouragingly and said, "Certainly, what are you making?"

"It's called '*Chocolate Mousse*'. Why I don't know because they don't look like any mouse I've ever seen. But oh well, that's the French for you. Anyway, they're in the fridge.

The sisters were finally able to settle down to a peaceful tea in happy contemplation of their successful afternoon at the police station. Jack arrived from London in time for dinner however Susana's unfortunate slip of the tongue in reply to her brother's question of how they had spent their day, put Jack in a foul mood which lasted throughout dinner and only abated when he exited before dessert saying he would spend the rest of the evening at the Raven's Roost.

"Well you really put your foot in it," admonished Cornelia as they sat enjoying Pinkey's dessert. "And another thing. Why didn't you tell me that the gong mallet was still missing? I assumed the change in tone was a Pinkey thing."

"I only just found out. Pinkey told me yesterday morning when I was looking for that funny shaped wooden spoon. Don't worry, we'll get used to the funny sound soon enough. Won't we?"

"That's not the point," replied Cornelia absently. "That mallet was probably the weapon that was used to hit Martha over the head. We're going to have to make a thorough search in the morning and I can only hope that Jack won't be around."

Arriving at the police station earlier than usual the next morning, Inspector Bunson was surprised to see Sergeant Rogers seated in front of his computer, his desk littered with papers which showed recent evidence of a 'venti' coffee.

"I couldn't sleep last night trying to make sense of all that the Leslies told us. I've been going over the timeline on the night Julia Peters was killed and added some bits and pieces to the data. If we stare at it long enough we might come up with something. Sorry about the coffee marks." He explained handing the papers to his superior.

DINNER PARTY TIMELINE UP TO DEATH OF JULIA PETERS

8:00pm:
- Cornelia and Jack Leslie having drinks in solarium;
- Susana in kitchen;
- Betty Smith not at manor;
- Martha Jenkins in kitchen peeling potatoes;
- Martha given orders to stay by door to await guests;
- Reverend Thomas Peters and Julia Peters first guests to arrive. Taken to solarium by Martha Jenkins;
- Phyllis Stavis and Debra O'Neil arrive. Use French windows at back terrace;
- Susana and Julia Peters leave solarium to find Martha;
- Sam Taylor arrives at front door;
- Moe Stone arrives immediately after Sam Taylor.

8:30pm:
- Susana rings dinner gong. Mallet discovered missing;
- Still no sign of Martha;
- Betty Smith arrives as hosts and guests are being seated in dining room.

9:30pm:
- Martha shows up in dining room, claims she was pushed down cellar stairs;
- Cornelia and Moe leave dining room to go to kitchen;
- Cornelia and Moe go back to dining room;
- Jack presents Julia with 'goblet of honor' with dessert wine;
- Cornelia leaves dining room to get Julia's tea;
- Jim McCarthy arrives;
- Cornelia goes back to dining room;
- Debra leaves dining room to get tea for Julia;
- Debra returns to dining room;
- Betty Smith leaves dining room for fresh pot of tea;
- Betty Smith returns to dining room;
- Betty Smith leaves dining room for coffee and fresh pot of tea;
- Betty Smith returns to dining room.

SEATING CHART

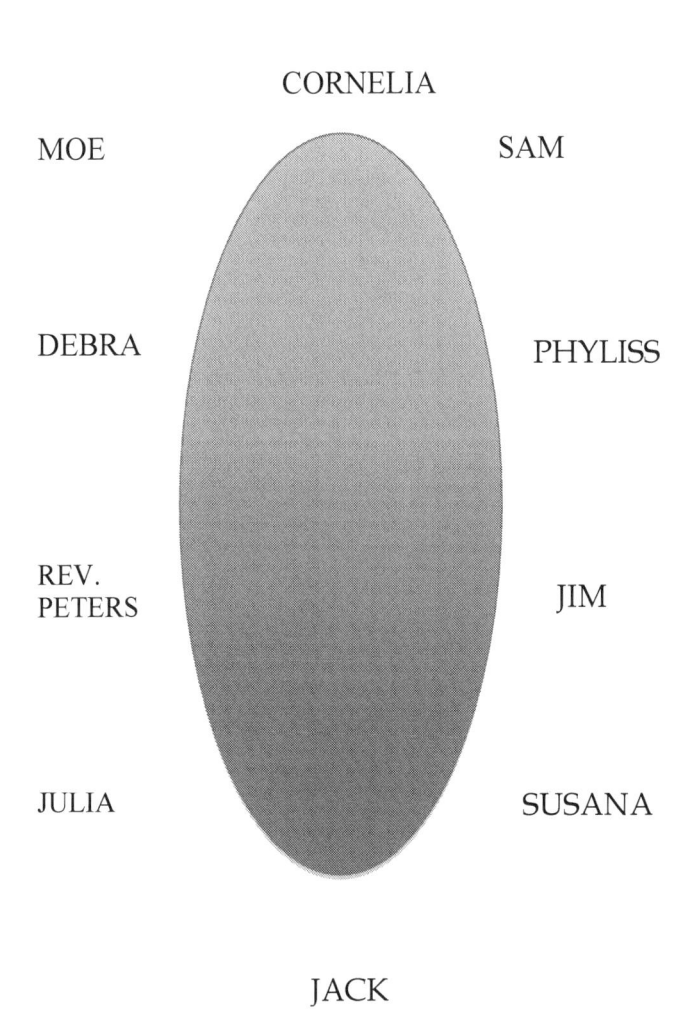

CORNELIA

MOE　　　　　　　　　　SAM

DEBRA　　　　　　　　PHYLISS

REV.
PETERS　　　　　　　　JIM

JULIA　　　　　　　　　SUSANA

JACK

Chapter 30

The Scotland Yard detectives spent the morning analyzing their notes and comparing them to the statements provided by the various parties. Midway through they received a call from a distressed Cornelia Leslie saying that she and Susana had forgotten to tell the police officers about Martha's speech to the Leslie household about knowing where something was hidden. At the time they assumed that it was another of Martha's weird performances but this morning they had found the dinner gong mallet under Martha's mattress. When they questioned Martha, they were told that she had found it lying next to her when she was pushed down the cellar stairs. She had kept it hidden anticipating another attack. The Leslie sisters feared that the two might have some connection albeit one which would involve prescience.

Cornelia was told that a constable would be sent to pick up the mallet after many reassurances that they had handled the mallet with the utmost care in order to preserve any fingerprints.

"This might be the opening we need," observed Sergeant Rogers optimistically.

The Chief Inspector gave a slight grin and thought back to his early years on the force wondering if he had ever been as optimistically expectant. Years of experience had taken its toll on his perspective. "Let's concentrate on the poison. Seems to me that anyone around here can get their hands on any number of poisons just by going outside and picking a few leaves."

"You're half right, Inspector. Strychnine isn't found in any plants around here - much too damp and cold. But, it's use as a pesticide for rats is extremely popular, especially with farmers."

"Oh lord luv a duck, you're a big help. So the fact that a bag of strychnine was found on vicarage property doesn't mean a thing. Anyone with a garden could have a bag lying around, is that it?"

"Well, yeah, kind of," replied a nonchalant Rogers with a shrug. Then perking up he added, "But that leaves only the people at the party as possible suspects because if we believe their statements, Julia Peters was fine one moment and dead the next. And you know how quickly a large dose of strychnine takes to produce fatal results. It could have been introduced into her food by someone but that's pretty risky, especially when the intended victim is fastidiously monitoring the food and beverage."

As things would have it, three felicitous occurrences took place that afternoon which would result in a break in the investigation.

First, the Chief Constable called to tell them that Betty Smith was showing favorable signs of a complete recovery so that the doctors were amenable to her being interviewed that same afternoon; thirdly, a culinary staffer who had been working the Leslie party had shown up at the police station and left a signed statements containing valuable evidence; and third, the lab results produced images of fingerprints just below those of Martha Jenkins' prints.

The afternoon and evening after Betty Smith's interview, the detectives spent time going through every facet of their investigations tying up loose ends. Afterwards, a final meeting with the Chief Constable was scheduled for one last brainstorming session.

When the serious business of dealing with details and technicalities of police evidentiary procedure were finished, Major Sandowne shook his head thoughtfully and said, "Frankly, I'm alarmed and saddened at how many people in this village had strong motives for doing away with Julia Peters. It's a tricky business when they all have the means and opportunity as well. I don't have to tell you that we don't run across that very often." He finished with a resigned sigh, "I suspect that's part and parcel of living in a small village."

"It took the Leslie sisters' astute observations to make that clear," remarked the Inspector giving credit where credit was due.

"Yep, their performance tonight at the manor will hopefully bring down the show – pardon the pun," replied the Sergeant.

Chapter 31

At a little before eight o'clock that evening, Cornelia nervously paced the solarium floor with a drink in her hand as her brother, Jack, sat quietly drinking his. While in the kitchen, Susana, covered in flour chattered anxiously with Pinkey. It was very difficult maintaining one's composure and pretending not to notice the constables in every room not to mention those outside.

A drawn looking Thomas Peters was the first to arrive. He was lead to the solarium by Martha Jenkins, now accustomed to her celebrity status in the village and using it to her best advantage. At present a London constable acted as full-time bodyguard. Next to arrive were Debra Singer and Phyllis Stavis, again as on the fateful night, entering through the French windows and Debra hiccuping uncontrollably. Meanwhile, Susana, with little clouds of flour billowing around her was cued to walk to the front hall in the presence of a constable. Sam Taylor stood by the door awaiting entry alongside Moe Stone. Constable Dibbs stood erect at the front door. Everyone gathered in the solarium but unlike the original dinner party, there were no sounds of ice against crystal nor was merry laughter heard. Aside from Debra's hiccuping, no one uttered a word at the party hosted by Scotland Yard. At the sound of the dinner gong – still rung with a wooden spoon – everyone entered the dining room and in response to the instructions given by Inspector Bunson sat in the same seating arrangement as on the night of the party. Those who could not remember their places were either reminded by the others or instructed by the police.. The police had imposed silence and nervous tension permeated the room. When all were seated, Martha walked into the dining room escorted by a young constable. Unlike her prior debut, Martha now strolled in and much to the dismay of the young constable who had been ordered to keep her quiet, entered humming loudly and only stopping when Sergeant Rogers' requested that she sit down next to him. Next, Cornelia and Moe Stone were escorted to the kitchen while Jack was asked to retrieve the 'goblet of honor' and place it at the place where Julia Peters had sat. Back in the dining room, Cornelia was prompted to answer the front door to an awaiting Jim McCarthy who was ineffectively attempting to get information from a silent Constable Dibbs. In the meantime, Debra was cued to the butler's pantry and back to the dining room. As Cornelia returned to the dining room, the door of which was now guarded by a constable, Betty was wheeled out into the hall by Sergeant Rogers and Inspector Bunson. They encountered Jim McCarthy just finishing his part in the scripted proceedings coming out of the butler's pantry. Upon seeing Betty his face turned ashen, contorted and then he lunged towards her only to be immediately pounced upon by two constables.

In the police car, having regained his

composure and declining the presence of a solicitor, Jim McCarthy signed a complete confession detailing his involvement in the crimes of first degree murder and assault with intent to commit murder.

The rest of the party spent a tortuous twenty minutes unaware of the happenings out in the back hall with Susana and Cornelia suffering the most by the police imposed silence while the murderer was being charged. To the astonishment of all those in the room the door was suddenly opened by Sergeant Rogers wheeling in a smiling and remarkably healthy looking Betty Smith wearing only a head scarf around her head. Inspector Bunson followed.

Susana ran up to the young woman saying, "Oh we're so glad you've recovered! We can't tell you how worried everyone was when we heard what happened. You're very brave to have gone out there to face him!" Changing her topic she said, "I'm famished, anyone else hungry?"

"Yes it's wonderful to see you, Betty. I'm so very sorry for everything you've been through," said the vicar his voice more shaky than usual. Walking over to Martha, who to everyone's alarm was uncharacteristically quiet said, "Martha, I owe you an apology for what happened to you. I wish I could have prevented it." Slowly shuffling back to his chair, he continued shakily, "I'm a silly old man who couldn't or wouldn't see the evil that was happening directly in front of him."

"Cocktails in the library everyone, that is if it's all right with the Inspector," Jack added hastily trying to relieve an uncomfortable silence.

"And we're serving supper in the solarium in thirty minutes!" added Susana happily.

"What about the maniac killer and why did we

have to do everything just like the other night?" exclaimed Martha only just noticing her bodyguard was no longer beside her.

"Could someone...hiccup...please explain what is...hiccup... going on here?" demanded Debra looking at Inspector Bunson.

"Surely, if you would all go to the library, Sergeant Rogers will give you an account of the last few days," replied the Inspector. Purposely walking to where the vicar was sitting he suggested to him that he might offer him a ride home only to be politely yet firmly turned down.

"Thank you Inspector but I've come to terms with the fact that Julia was a particularly unpleasant person. Now I have to face the people she so wickedly abused."

Everyone was comfortably settled with drinks in the library however they were still too dumbfounded for unstilted conversation.

Sergeant Rogers stood in the background observing the people around whom he had lived most of his life. The past few days had been a blight on the village and the residents had suffered knowing that someone they possibly knew had committed a heinous crime. He was taken out of his thoughts when Phyllis yelled to him to stop wasting time and get on with the story.

The following is a recounting of Scotland Yard's summation of the case.

Julia Peters and Jim McCarthy had met in the south of France several years earlier when she was on vacation with her brother. Shortly after his wife's death Jim had decided to leave London and go to

France. Not knowing the language and being unfamiliar with the foreign customs he was out of sorts in a strange land, and was easy prey for Julia who took him under her wing for the two weeks that they spent together in France. Still reeling from the blow of his wife's untimely death and the desperation it brought him, it was easy to capitulate to Julia's overtures. He eventually gave way with a proposal of marriage. But Julia being Julia would not make things simple. She had other plans. He would have to move to the village in Epping where they would pretend to not know each other and they would begin their relationship anew. She delighted in visions of flaunting him in front of the villagers and began an aggressive campaign for the move to Epping baiting him with the allure of starting a paper in the town – which she would fund. His small savings had been foolishly invested making Julia's offer all the more enticing.

Once back in England he spent a day scouting the village. It didn't take him long to convince himself that the tranquility and beauty of the countryside would help him adjust to the loss of his wife. He accepted Julia's offer.

The newspaper that Julia Peters secretly funded and which Jim McCarthy ran, quickly gained in popularity and subscriptions rose at a steady pace. Soon the paper was seen as an invaluable asset to the town and village with its editor becoming a prominent citizen. Everything was going according to Julia's plan and she became more and more persistent not only about marriage but the management of the paper itself. With the success of the paper, Jim McCarthy was happy again, pouring all his time and energy into the business while at the same time ignoring Julia.

Furious at her lover's independent attitude, Julia threatened to remove him as editor and expose him as a fraud. It was then that he planned the London weekends in an effort to stall her, staying in large hotels where it was easy to blend in. The more time he spent with her the less marriage seemed an option and he was able to forestall her with a taste of London nightlife which she had never before experienced.

One night when Julia and Jim were at a nightclub in London, eagle-eyed Julia noticed that Betty Smith was sitting at a table with several friends. Betty had been earnestly watching them and seemed amused by their behavior and Julia's drinking. Julia became incensed and agitated. How would they explain this? They would have to call Betty over and explain that they were celebrating their engagement and that they had not wanted to tell anyone in the village until they had made a formal announcement. Later, Jim McCarthy would be thankful for this last comment.

As editor of the town newspaper Jim McCarthy had access to most of the village's inside politics. He had carelessly told Julia about Sam Taylor's new business venture and his wish to purchase land from the Leslies. It was well known that Sam Taylor's position as chairman of the Board of Selectman was a thorn in Julia's side and that she used Moe Stone, a member of the board as a tool to impede Sam's influence on the board and further hers. It was a competitive game to obstruct Sam Taylor that gave her immense pleasure and so, without hesitating, Julia contacted the Leslies with a subtle hint of donating land for the expansion of the cemetery.

The invitation to the Leslie manor for the announcement of the donation of land was at first, an irritation for Jim McCarthy. He could hear Julia hounding him that it would be the perfect time for their 'announcement'. He was right. She not only hounded him, she demanded that he purchase a ring – or else. She had prepared the notice that he would 'proudly' recite at the end of dinner.

Little by little a plan began to form in Jim McCarthy's mind as a possible way to remove Julia's suffocating stronghold. On one of his innocuous visits to the vicarage, he had spotted a bag of strychnine in the potting shed. A few grains of the deadly poison killed rats. He did his research and found out that strychnine is odorless and can be easily mixed in a solution. More importantly, results were rapid, fifteen minutes at most. Having decided on the agent of death, he now focused on the method. Why not let Julia's farce of never imbibing be her demise? The foul tea bags she carried in her purse to every village function would be the perfect foil! He now looked forward with anticipation to the Leslie dinner party.

Once he had made up his mind, the rest was ridiculously easy. At first, he acquiesced to Julia's arrangements that they arrive together to the party. However on the evening of the party, he called Julia at the last second with the pretext that he had been called out to a fire in the next town and she would have to go ahead with her brother. He would meet her at the manor in time for the big moment. In truth, he arrived at the manor well ahead of Julia and her brother and waited hidden in the shrubbery near the dining room French windows. Here he remained until the time when dessert would be served and when

Julia habitually drank her tea. Then he quickly made his way to the front door and when Cornelia greeted him he apologized with a story of a prank phone call. With a stroke of luck, Cornelia told him that Julia had demanded her tea and that she was going into the kitchen to ask that it be laid out in the butler's pantry. Jim responded saying he wanted to use the men's room to wash up. He waited until Cornelia had gone back to the dining room then he entered the pantry and reaching into his jacket pocket, quickly took one of the two bags lying on a tray and replaced it with one he had carefully doctored with strychnine. He knew that Julia always used two bags. Once in the dining room, it was easy sailing. He just acted like one of the guests carefully avoiding eye contact with Julia who by now was in such a foul temper that she was turning purple. "Or was that the effect of the strychnine?" he had happily wondered to himself.

At this point Sergeant Rogers proceeded to recount the evidence that Scotland Yard had collected with the assistance from the Leslie sisters. At the time the culinary staff had been interviewed, no information was obtained that could lead to any possible clue. However, a few days later, a staffer had come into the police station saying that he recalled seeing a man enter the butler's pantry for just a couple of seconds. At the time, he didn't think anything of it because he figured it was a guest looking for a bathroom. When he read about the murderer having used poison, it jarred his memory. Then the police lab definitively confirmed that there were traces of strychnine in Julia's teacup. Thanks to some fine sleuthing by the Leslies, the jacket that Jim McCarthy had worn on the night of the party had been analyzed with the result that small traces of tea and strychnine had been found in one of the pockets. This would not necessarily be admissible in a court of law but for one very fortunate occurrence – the recovery of Betty Smith who not only verified Jim McCarthy's London story, but also identified her assailant as the same person. Aware of the secret relationship between Jim McCarthy and Julia Peters, Betty suspected Jim of having the best motive for doing away with Julia. At first she was frightened to death with the probability but later she decided that it could prove financially advantageous. The day after the inquest, she called the editor and arranged to meet him at his office to discuss a mutually beneficial agreement. They agreed to meet the following day. Acquainted with the route that Betty would take into the village, Jim McCarthy accosted her on the footpath along Hunter's Bosk. Finally, Martha had indeed been shoved down the cellar stairs but not by Jim McCarthy. The perpetrator had been Julia Peters. Essentially, Martha had unknowingly found Julia's diary hidden under the alter cloths in the church vestry. However, being almost illiterate, she had no idea of it's content. Naively, she went to the person in charge of alter decorations, and presented her newly discovered treasure. The paroxysms of rage on Julia's face along with her insistence that Martha tell no one, frightened Martha so much that she decided she had indeed found a long lost treasure. Hence, the statements of '*I know where it's 'idden'*. On the evening of the Leslie party, Martha had been upset at being relegated from potato peeler to door opener and decided that she was very tired and needed a rest. She knew there was a cot in the cellar where she could lie down and by keeping the door open she'd still be able to hear the front door bell. Just as she had accommodated herself comfortably, the doorbell rang. She got up but the silly apron she was forced to wear had disappeared. Rushing to answer the door, she found the apron at the top of the stairs. That was the last she remembered until she woke on the floor of the cellar with the dinner gong mallet lying beside her. The fact that Julia Peters' fingerprints were found below those of Martha's was proof that she had been the person behind the attack.

Chapter 32

Having finished the last report and turning it over to a very pleased Major Sandowne, the two detectives got into the police car and headed back to London.

"Who ever said living in a small country village was boring didn't know what they were talking about!" remarked a tired Inspector Bunson with mixed feelings about going back to the City.

"C'mon Inspector, it's got it's pros and cons just like the city. They're just a little more concentrated in a village," replied Sergeant Rogers grinning.

"I don't think I'll sleep a wink tonight with everything that's happened. Imagine! We helped Scotland Yard catch a murderer! Amazing isn't it?" exclaimed Susana fluffing up her pillows with a satisfied sigh.

"Not really. We've always been very good listeners. Detective work is right up our alley!" replied Cornelia feet up on the divan as usual and sipping her Ovaltine.

EPILOGUE

Julia Peters' diary was found hidden in her bedroom vanity recounting her affair with Jim McCarthy.

BANGERS and MASH
As served at the Ravens Roost Pub

8 English bangers or Kosher beef knockwurst
6 large russet potatoes cut into quarters
½ to 1 cup cream or milk
5 TBSP butter
salt to taste
3 cups frozen peas
good quality steak sauce

    Heat water to boiling in a large pot. When boiling, add salt and potatoes and cook until soft (approx. 20 minutes). Drain the potatoes and return to pot adding the cream or milk, 4 TBSP of the buttter, and salt to taste. Stir to mix. Meanwhile, using a grill pan, grill the bangers or knockwurst until nicely browned on all sides. Heat the peas according to package instructions.
    To serve: Plate individual plates with the mashed potatoes in the center and the bangers and peas around the potatoes. Serve with steak sauce.

Serves 8

OH GREAT TIN POTATOES
As served at Blandings Manor
(also known as Au Gratin Potatoes)

8 Yukon potatoes, peeled and sliced thinly
2 cups half and half
8 oz. shredded Jack cheese (2 cups)
1 tsp. thyme (fresh or dried)
salt and pepper to taste

Preheat oven to 375° degrees. In a large bowl, mix the potatoes, half and half, 1 cup of cheese and seasonings and layer in a greased casserole dish. Sprinkle remaining cheese on top. Bake for 2 hours.

Serves 8

CHOCOLATE MOUSES
as served at Blandings Manor
(also known as Chocolate Mousse)

1 lb. semisweet chocolate, cut into small pieces
2 TBSP unsalted butter
1 cup sugar
6 egg yolks
6 egg whites
6 TBSP Marsala or good brandy

In a heatproof bowl, combine the chocolate, butter and 1/2 cup of sugar. Place in microwave for 30 seconds until chocolate is ALMOST melted. Remove and stir. Add the egg yolks and Marsala.
Beat the egg whites until stiff peaks form. Gradually beat in the remaining sugar and continue beating until stiff. When done whisk in 1/3 of egg whites into the chocolate mixture. Fold the chocolate mixture into the remaining whites with a wooden spoon. Pour the chocolate mixture into individual dessert bowls and refrigerate for 2 to 3 hours.

Serves 8

BUBBLE and SQUEAK
As served at the Tarts and Buns Teashop

4 mashed potatoes
½ of a cooked cabbage
3 TBSP butter
salt and pepper to taste

Spray a saute pan with non-stick spray. In a large bowl, mix the potatoes and cabbage and season to taste. Over medium heat melt the butter in a pan swirling so that the bottom of the pan is covered. Add the potato-cabbage mixture pressing down on the vegetables with a spatula. Cook until bottom is golden and then turn and brown on reverse side. Serve immediately.

Serves 6

SHEPHERD'S PIE
As served at the Tarts and Buns Teashop

2 to 2 ½ lbs. minced or ground lamb or beef
4 cups leftover mashed potatoes
1 cup frozen peas
1 cup frozen pearl onions
1 carrot, peeled and diced
1 ½ cups chicken broth
1 TBSP cumin
2 tsp. coriander
1 tsp. tumeric
1 tsp. salt
1 TBSP cornstarch
½ cup cold water
½ tsp. dried thyme
½ tsp. dried marjoram
¼ tsp. paprika

Preheat oven to 400º degrees. In a saute pan brown the lamb or beef. Add the sliced carrots, peas, onions and seasonings. Saute for about 2 minutes. Add broth and heat until bubbly. Simmer for 10 minutes or until vegetables are tender. In a small bowl mix the water and cornstarch and stir into mixture. Cook, stirring constantly until thickened. Remove from heat and transfer to a pie pan or Pyrex dish.
Cover with the potatoes and sprinkle top with paprika. Bake uncovered for 15 minutes. Serves 8

MRS. HARDY'S SHORTBREAD COOKIES
As served at the vicarage

1 cup unsalted butter, softened
1 cup sugar
1 egg
2 ½ cups flour
2 tsp. orange juice
1 tsp. vanilla
1 tsp. baking powder

    In a mixing bowl, mix 1 cup of butter, the sugar and egg. Beat until smooth. Add the rest of the ingredients and beat until mixed. Turn dough onto table and divide into three parts. Roll each section into a 12 inch roll. Wrap individually and refrigerate until firm. Heat oven to 400° degrees. Cut each roll into 1/4 inch thick rounds and place on cookie sheet. Bake for 10 minutes.

Makes about 2 dozen cookies.

MARROW (or ZUCCHINI) AND VEGETABLE SOUP
As served at the Vicarage

1 marrow or 2 large zucchini, chopped
2 carrots, chopped
1 sweet onion, chopped
1 russet potato, chopped
6 cups vegetable broth
3 TBSP butter
1 inch piece fresh ginger, peeled and chopped
1 TBSP fresh cilantro, chopped
1 jalapeno pepper, chopped
½ cup cream
¼ tsp. nutmeg
salt and pepper to taste

Heat a large soup pot and melt the butter. Add all the vegetables and saute, stirring, until tender. Do not burn. When done, add broth and bring to a boil. Simmer on low for ten minutes. Take off heat and let cool slightly. Pour contents of pot into a blender or food processor and blend to a smooth consistency or to taste. Return to pot adding cream, nutmeg, cilantro and salt and pepper. Gently warm.

Serves 6

Printed in Great Britain
by Amazon